The Year of the Hangman

Other books by
GARY BLACKWOOD

The Shakespeare Stealer

Shakespeare's Scribe

Wild Timothy

Moonshine

The Year of the Hangman

GARY BLACKWOOD

SCHOLASTIC INC.

New York   Toronto   London   Auckland   Sydney
Mexico City   New Delhi   Hong Kong   Buenos Aires

ISBN 0-439-63626-4

Published by Scholastic Inc., 557 Broadway, New York, NY 10012,
by arrangement with Dutton Childrens's Books,
a member of Penguin Group (USA) Inc. SCHOLASTIC and associated
logos are trademarks and/or registered trademarks of Scholastic Inc.

12 11 10 9 8 7 6 5 4 3   4 5 6 7 8 9/0

Printed in the U.S.A.   40

First Scholastic printing, April 2004

Designed by Gloria Cheng

For Phil, Ophelia, Naomi,
and all the others who bring writers
and readers together

By the winter of 1776, the American Revolution seemed doomed. The Continental Army had suffered major defeats at Quebec and Long Island, and again at Fort Washington, where more than three hundred American officers and four thousand enlisted men were taken prisoner. General Washington was under personal attack. On one hand, the British were plotting to kill or capture him; on the other, many of his countrymen—even some of his own officers—were calling for him to resign. Even if he stayed on, he was in imminent danger of losing his army. Most of the soldiers had enlisted for only one year, and their time was nearly up.

As we all know, Washington managed to beat the odds against him. He convinced his men to reenlist, launched a surprise attack on Trenton, and went on to defeat the British.

But it didn't have to happen that way. The course of history often hinges on very small events. If any one of a dozen things had taken a slightly different turn—if Washington had been captured or killed, if the militiamen had chosen to go home instead of reenlisting, if the British commander at Trenton had heeded the warning he received of the Americans' attack—the outcome might have been very different.

This is a story of what might have happened.

The Year of the Hangman

Chapter ONE

At least once a week, Creighton Brown's mother predicted that he would come to a bad end. Though she never specified what she meant by "a bad end," it was understood to mean the end of a hangman's rope.

Creighton paid little mind to his mother's warnings. Like most wellborn English lads, he had grown up regarding death by hanging not as a cruel and dreadful fate so much as a form of amusement.

When Creighton was twelve, he and his schoolmates had played almost obsessively at a game they called Hangman. There were two players. One was the Hangman; he drew on his slate a crude gallows that resembled a large number 7, then selected as his victim some well-known public figure—James Bruce, the explorer, for example, or Lord North. The other player had to guess the identity of the

condemned man. Each time he guessed wrong, the Hangman suspended a body part from the gallows—a circle for
the head, simple lines for arms and legs. If the other player
guessed correctly before the stick figure was complete, he
won a reprieve for the victim and became the Hangman
himself.

After the troubles with the Colonies began, the player
who was Hangman often chose for his victim some notori-
ous American—the rabble-rousing Sam Adams, perhaps,
or Benjamin Franklin, who was in London at the time, ar-
guing the American cause. This was a clever ploy, for, if
the other player suspected that the victim was a Yankey,
he usually preferred to let the rascal hang.

When he was thirteen, Creighton attended his first real-
life execution, skipping his classes to do so. The condemned was the celebrated highwayman Tom Corbett,
who had been making the road from Bristol to London
unsafe for travelers for more than a year.

The execution had been well publicized by means of
handbills, and hundreds of eager spectators, some with
young children in tow, flocked to the courtyard before the
jail, hoping for a satisfying show. Corbett did not disappoint them. The highwayman, who was tall, good-looking,
and not much over twenty years of age, played to the
crowd like a seasoned actor.

When the clergyman asked whether there was anything
that might comfort him, the thief coolly replied, "Having
another man hang in my place." The crowd applauded.
When the noose was placed about his neck, Corbett did

not wait to be pushed from the scaffold; with a cry of "A short life, and a merry one!" he leaped into space.

Though the sight of the dangling body haunted Creighton for weeks, the thing that impressed itself most indelibly on his memory was the dashing, devil-may-care manner in which the highwayman had met his fate.

In 1777, the year that Creighton turned fifteen, hanging became a familiar topic of conversation. Some even called it the Year of the Hangman, because the three sevens in the date resembled miniature gallows, and also because the year had begun with a rash of executions. In one fortnight, in London, thirteen men were strung up on the scaffold at Tyburn. They were not the usual run of thieves and murderers, but respectable men of substance. Some were merchants, some government officials; one was a member of Parliament. All were traitors to the crown, convicted of selling supplies or secrets to the rebels during the short-lived and ill-fated uprising in America.

Creighton was too busy to notice. Though he was still enrolled in school, it wasn't his studies that occupied him. In fact he seldom cracked a book, and was absent from his classes more often than not—usually because he was sleeping off the excesses of the night before.

Most of his education came not in the classroom but in coffeehouses and taverns, and his teachers were the town's rakes and wastrels—for the most part, the younger sons of wealthy fathers. As they had no property to manage and no trade to pursue, they made a profession out of drinking, smoking, and playing cards.

Creighton was an eager apprentice to the profession. Even before his father, a career soldier, went off to the Colonies to help keep the rebels in hand, Creighton had shown a tendency toward "running wild," as his mother put it. The mischief he indulged in was mostly minor—stealing fruit at the market; setting off fireworks under Sir Ambrose Spencer's privy (while it was occupied by Sir Ambrose); digging up Captain Granville's yard in search of the treasure rumored to be buried there.

Major Brown's influence had kept his son's behavior within acceptable bounds. But with his father off in America, Creighton quickly stepped out of bounds and fell under less wholesome influences. His grandfather, Sir Robert, declared that the boy needed something to occupy his time and his mind and offered to have him apprenticed to a solicitor or a physician. But Charlotte Brown would have none of it. She meant for her son to be a gentleman, and a gentleman, by her definition, was someone who didn't have to work for a living—a notion that appealed strongly to Creighton.

Unfortunately, a gentleman *was* expected to have a classical education, and that meant a good deal of study, which definitely did not appeal to Creighton. Most of his troubles at school, though, came about not because he hated studying, but because he hated authority of any sort, especially when it was unjust. Though most of the other students admired his defiant attitude, the authorities of course despised it, and it had managed to get him booted out of two prestigious academies—so far.

At the first, one of the masters had tried to punish him for breaking some minor rule; Creighton had broken the man's cane. At the second, Creighton had stood up for a classmate, a rather pitiful fellow with one withered arm, who was being tormented by a bully. Creighton had given the lout a bloody nose. Unfortunately the bully's father proved to be an earl who had contributed large sums of money to the school, and he demanded that Creighton be dismissed.

His current school was not as exclusive as the first two. The parents of his new classmates tended to have less money and fewer titles. Some of the fathers were not even gentlemen, but mere merchants. Though the tobacco trade was the source of his own family's wealth, Creighton looked down upon these working-class boys—and, in fact, on most of the students. They all seemed so dull, so childish, compared with the dashing young men who met in the taverns nightly to squander their share of the family fortune on drinks and gaming. Creighton liked their elegant manners, their bawdy wit, their carefree outlook on life—an outlook whose basic premise seemed to be that the world had been created expressly for their pleasure.

There was a time when the person he most admired was his own father—and with good reason. Major Brown was everything an officer and gentleman should be, but seldom is: intelligent, capable, compassionate, honorable, courageous. But his father was dead now, killed in a skirmish with rebels in a place called Carolina. The one quality Harry Brown had lacked was luck.

In this respect, Creighton took after his father—at least where games of chance were concerned. He had once thought himself clever at cards. He had played whist regularly with his mother and her friends, and he and his partner invariably won. Now he suspected that he had been allowed to win—that his mother had, as usual, been catering to his whims, afraid that if he lost, it would put him in a bad temper.

His tavern companions did not play whist; their game of choice was single-stake brag, and their bets were reckoned in pounds not pence. Unlike his mother, they did not cater to him or commiserate with him, no matter how badly he lost. They seemed utterly unconcerned about money, so it was all one to them whether they won or lost.

Creighton tried to be as nonchalant as they were. As he watched the last of his month's allowance being raked from the table, he gave what he hoped was a careless laugh and took a long draught of ale to ease the tightness in his throat. "Well, gentlemen, that's all the cash I have on me, I'm afraid. But I feel my fortunes are about to take a turn for the better. I presume you'll accept a chit from me?"

The other three players glanced at one another. Gilbert Burke, his broad face flushed with drink, shrugged good-naturedly. "If the lad wants to lose his breeches as well as his purse, I say let him."

Roger Davy nodded in agreement. "I've no doubt he's good for it. If nothing else, he can pay us in kind, with sot-weed from his grandfather's warehouse, eh?"

Only Thomas Kern, Creighton's closest companion among the men, and the nearest to him in age, seemed doubtful. He drew Creighton aside. "Are you certain you can afford to lose any more, Cray?"

Creighton smiled thinly. "I don't intend to lose."

"No one ever does. Pardon me for pointing this out, but you're not exactly known for your shrewdness at betting."

"It's a matter of luck, that's all," Creighton replied indignantly, "and mine is bound to change eventually. In any case, it's only money, isn't it? And my family has plenty of that."

This was not quite true. In fact, their financial situation was shaky at best. For reasons known only to the army, his mother had not yet received any of her husband's pension. They could not depend on Harry's father for much help, either. When the troubles with the Colonies began, Sir Robert's profits had dwindled drastically, partly because the tobacco trade was suspended and partly because several ships full of other cargo were seized by American privateers.

Creighton suspected that, in order to maintain the style of life her place in society demanded, his mother was accepting loans from gentleman admirers, such as Sir Edward Lyndon, who called upon her almost daily. Creighton considered these visits and loans improper, especially since his father had been dead for little more than a year.

Though his friend Thomas no doubt knew all this, he didn't press the issue; it was considered bad form for gentlemen to quibble over money matters. But Thomas did add softly, "They'll expect you to make good your debts, you know. It's not that they care about the money. It's a question of honor, and though this lot may seem easygoing, when honor is involved it's no longer a game; it's serious business."

"I can handle myself," Creighton replied, but the boast had a hollow sound.

"I hope so," muttered Thomas as they returned to the table.

To Creighton's relief, his luck did seem to take a turn for the better. He was dealt an ace of hearts and a nine of diamonds, which was a "bragger," or wild card—the equivalent of a pair of aces. Gilbert led off the betting with a marker for half a crown. The others put in an equal amount. Confident that he held a winning hand, Creighton raised the bet; he wrote *five shillings* on a scrap of paper, initialed it, and tossed it into the center of the table. The others saw his raise; then it was Creighton's turn again.

This time he put in a chit for a pound. Gilbert glanced up at him in surprise. Though he knew he shouldn't let his face betray him, Creighton couldn't help smiling a bit smugly. Gilbert smiled, too, and tossed markers worth thirty shillings into the pot. Roger matched it; so did Thomas.

Creighton raised his bet to two pounds. Gilbert followed suit. Roger folded his cards and tossed them aside. "I know when I'm outgunned." He rose from the table. "Can I fetch anyone another pint?"

"Give me a moment," Creighton said, "and I'll have the money for it."

Roger laughed. "We'll see."

After another round of betting, Thomas dropped out. "You may want to give it up now, lad," Gilbert warned good-naturedly, "before you go so far out on a limb that you hang yourself."

Creighton was sure the man was bluffing. Though his palms were perspiring so that he could scarcely hold the cards, he managed a credible smile. "I'm not at the end of my rope just yet." Shakily he scribbled another chit, for three pounds this time. He heard Thomas groan, but he didn't take his eyes off Gilbert's cards, as though staring at them would reveal their worth, or perhaps cause them to fold.

But instead of folding, Gilbert tossed three one-guinea markers on the pile. "No point in prolonging the agony. I'll call." He spread his cards face up on the table. "Two royal ladies, natural. I hope for your sake you can better that."

Anger welled up in Creighton, and before he could stop himself, he had flung his hand down petulantly. The others stared at him in astonishment, as though he'd done something unforgivably gauche. Embarrassed and ashamed, Creighton murmured, "No. I can't better it."

"Pity." Gilbert raked the pile of coins and paper into his hat. "I'll buy the next round, gentlemen."

Creighton took a deep, trembling breath and got unsteadily to his feet. "You'll forgive me if I don't accept. I have classes in a few hours, and should allow myself a little sleep first." He bowed slightly to Gilbert. "May I have a day or two to make good my debt, sir?"

Gilbert waved a hand indulgently. "By all means. You won't expect to play again, I know, before the matter is settled."

"Naturally not." Creighton donned his cloak and fastened it. "Good night, gentlemen." There was no reply. The three men were already engaged in some conversation that did not include him.

Outside the tavern Creighton drew his cloak close around him. The air was chilly for April, and a mist hung in the air, forming halos around the gas lamps on the street corners. Creighton made his way home through the narrow alleys, away from the glow of the lamps. It was long past curfew, and he didn't care to run afoul of the city's watchmen. He had troubles enough.

By the time he reached his home, he had worked out how he would repay the six pounds five he owed. His mother's stock of jewelry was so extensive, she wouldn't miss a particular necklace or brooch, at least not for several weeks. That would give him plenty of time to raise more money so he could redeem the items from the pawnbroker. And if he didn't . . . well, he could disavow any knowledge of the jewelry's fate, and very likely his mother would believe him. It had worked before.

But she had grown more suspicious lately, and less tolerant of his transgressions. When she had discovered that he was slipping out of the house at night, she had instructed the maid to lock him in his room. Creighton had simply climbed out the window. Next she had tried locking all the doors and windows while he was out, to teach him a lesson. Furious, Creighton had gained entry by smashing a windowpane and unfastening the lock.

He hoped she would try no such nonsense tonight, for he was bone weary and didn't want the bother of breaking in. The house was dark. She wasn't waiting up, then, and there would be no lectures about how disappointed she was in him, or about how he was dishonoring his father's memory.

Creighton plodded up the steps to the front door and fished about in his pocket for the iron key. As he softly inserted the key into the lock, he heard the boards of the porch creak behind him, and he half turned, puzzled by the sound.

A pair of hands seized his arms, pinning them behind his back, and a stout arm clamped around his neck, forcing his head back. He opened his mouth to cry out, but a crumpled cloth was crammed between his teeth, then another cloth was pulled tight over it and tied in place. Before he could get a glimpse of his assailants, a third band of fabric was put over his eyes.

Squirming frantically, he lashed out with his legs at the attackers. There was a muttered curse as one of the kicks connected. Something solid struck him hard on the right knee and he doubled over in pain, with a gasp that drew the ball of cloth into his throat, gagging him. As a final indignity, his wrists were bound together, like a condemned man's, with rough cord. Then he was half carried, half dragged from the porch and off into the night.

———◆◆◆◆———

Chapter TWO

T hough Creighton was larger than most boys his age, his idle existence had left him soft and weak, and the hands that gripped his arms and clutched the back of his coat were unyielding. After a few moments he gave up struggling and concentrated on staying on his feet. When he failed, the hands jerked him mercilessly upright and forced him on.

The cold, damp air creeping down his neck made him shudder and hunch his shoulders. He had lost his cloak during the scuffle, and his damask coat and silk waistcoat had been fashioned with style, not warmth, in mind.

His captors gave no clue to their identity or their intent. They spoke not a word, except for the occasional epithet when Creighton balked or stumbled. Now and again he heard a clink of metal that he took to be the rattling of a sword hilt. These men were not common ruffians, then; swords were carried only by gentlemen.

But what could they hope to gain by abducting him? A ransom, perhaps? Or might this have something to do with his gambling losses? There had been other losses before tonight, and he hadn't always made good on them. Were these some old creditors, then, exacting vengeance on him?

A dog barked ahead of them, sounding muffled in the fog, and a voice called, "Who goes?" Creighton gasped again, this time with relief. He promptly gagged on the wad of cloth, but he scarcely minded. Here was hope, in the form of a night watchman.

A lone watchman with a pike and a dog was no match for two men armed with rapiers, of course, especially if this fellow was like most of the city's watch—decrepit old men who could find no other line of work. But once the man saw that mischief was afoot, he would certainly fetch a constable.

Creighton heard the watchman's shuffling footsteps and the low growl of his mastiff. "What's this?" the man demanded. "What d'you think you're doing, there?" One of the kidnappers released his hold on Creighton's arm and moved forward to confront the watchman. "Oh, it's you, sir!" The watchman's tone was suddenly all courtesy and no challenge.

There followed an exchange of words too low for Creighton to make out. Then, to his dismay, his free arm was seized once more, and he was sent stumbling forward. He flung his head about wildly, hoping to dislodge the gag enough so he could cry out for help. It was useless. Tears of frustration stung his eyes and wetted the cloth of his blindfold.

Even in his distraught state, he noticed that the surface beneath his feet had changed from cobbles to bricks. That meant they were near the waterfront, a fact that was confirmed by the familiar smells of fish and tar that hung in the air.

His captors paused, as though looking about for something, then urged him on. One man walked ahead of him now, and one behind him, keeping a secure hold on the cord that bound his wrists. He was guided up a slight incline, and their footsteps echoed on wooden planks—a gangway. They were taking him aboard a ship.

He had heard of men and boys being abducted and pressed into service on Royal Navy vessels, but the victims were always lower-class louts—drunks and orphans and the like—never lads from good families. This was clearly a mistake, one that would certainly be put right once he revealed who he was and who his family were, a mistake that his captors would have reason to regret.

They were conversing with someone again, but the words were obscured by the ever-present sounds of the harbor: the creaking of spars, the plash of water against the ship's hull, the thump of smaller boats nudging the pilings of the wharf, the clang of a bell buoy far out in the channel.

Creighton prepared to release a torrent of indignation the moment his gag was removed. But it wasn't removed. He was seized by the collar of his coat and shoved across the gently shifting deck of the ship. He tried to scream a protest, but succeeded only in gagging himself again.

His shoulder collided with something solid, sending a jolt of pain through his already aching body. Then he was pushed down onto a pad or mattress with a wooden frame that scraped the backs of his knees—a bunk, he imagined.

"I can't cut you loose just yet," said a gruff voice, "but I can take the gag out if you promise not to make a fuss."

Creighton nodded once, impatiently. Hands fumbled with the fabric around his mouth, untied it. He spat out the ball of cloth and shouted hoarsely, "Help! Ho! I'm be-ing—" The words were cut off by a blow to his face. As he slumped forward, groaning, the band of cloth was jammed between his jaws and tied in place so tightly that his teeth punctured the insides of his cheeks.

"There, now!" said the voice, sounding a bit out of breath. "Since you won't behave yourself, you may chew on that a while longer." There were footfalls, then the sound of a heavy wooden door being shut and locked.

Disoriented and dizzy with exhaustion, Creighton sank onto his side on the mattress and drew his knees up. He knew he needed to take some action before it was too late, before the ship set sail. If he worked free of his bonds, he might find a way to escape; failing that, he could pound on the door of his prison and protest at the top of his lungs until someone listened.

But for the moment he couldn't find the strength or the will even to move, so he only lay there, moaning softly and now and again swallowing the blood that seeped from the cuts in his mouth.

He was awakened by someone removing the blindfold from his eyes. Startled, Creighton tried to sit up and nearly passed out from the pain that coursed through his skull. At first he thought he'd been struck again, on the pate this time. Then he recognized the real source of the pain, as one recognizes an old enemy: It was the crapulence brought on by drinking too much ale.

There was light beyond his closed eyelids. He forced them open, flinching as the light struck his dark-accustomed eyes. He had been aboard his grandfather's ships enough times to know that the cramped room was an officer's cabin.

"You look like a heap of offal," said the gruff voice. "Want a drink?"

Creighton tilted his head to take in a beefy, rough-looking man sitting on a bunk a few feet away. Though he looked more like a sheep farmer than a gentleman, he wore the uniform of a Marine guard lieutenant. The man poured an inch or so of amber liquid from a flask. "Drink?" he repeated, enunciating clearly and indicating the glass in his hand, as though he were speaking to some-one foreign or perhaps feebleminded.

Creighton nodded, very carefully lest his head fall off. He sat up again, more slowly this time. The room seemed to be swaying around him. It took him a moment to realize

that he wasn't imagining it; the ship was rocking rhythmically. He glanced out the small window next to him
and saw nothing but water. Alarmed, he sprang to his feet,
hit his head on the low ceiling, and abruptly sat down
again.

"You may as well save your strength," said the lieutenant. "You'll not be getting off this ship now—not until
we reach the Colonies."

"The Colonies?" Creighton echoed in dismay; the cloth
gag reduced the words to incoherent grunts.

"I suppose we can remove that now, if you mind your
manners. It's no good shouting, anyway, as there's no one
to hear you—no one who will care." The man leaned
across the narrow aisle between the bunks, untied the
cloth, and held the glass to Creighton's bruised lips.
Creighton drank greedily, then choked and spat most of it
out as it burned his parched throat and his lacerated
cheeks. "Here, don't be wasting good kill-devil, my lad."
The man poured another shot and downed it in one gulp,
as if to show how it should be done.

When the stinging in his throat subsided, Creighton
rasped, "I demand to speak to the captain at once."

The officer gave a bark of a laugh. "You *demand* it, do
you? Well, the captain's busy."

"You don't understand," Creighton went on, keeping a
reasonable tone despite the anger and frustration that
threatened to overwhelm him. "This is all a mistake. I'm
certain of it. If I could just talk to him—"

"What's your name?" the officer interrupted.

"Creighton Brown. My father is Major Harry Brown. My grandfather is Sir Robert Brown."

"There's no mistake, then. You're the very one they wanted."

"*They?*" Creighton shouted. "Who is *they?*"

The beefy man raised a threatening hand. "Careful how you address me, my lad, or I'll slap you down again."

Creighton replied spitefully, "No gentleman would strike another who cannot defend himself."

"Is that so?" The officer yanked a dagger from a sheath at his belt and, seizing one of Creighton's arms, jerked it toward him. Creighton grimaced, certain the man meant to cut him. But the blade sliced only the cords that bound his wrists. "There. Now you can defend yourself, eh?"

"I would, if I had a sword." Creighton flexed his hands to get some feeling back into them. "And if I could hold one."

"Yes, well, I'm not likely to just hand over a sword to a prisoner, now, am I?"

"Is that what I am? A prisoner?"

"For the moment. My instructions are to let you loose once we're well out of reach of any landfall."

"Your instructions? It wasn't you who abducted me, then?"

"What would I want with you? I'm in charge of the ship's Marine guard, that's all. It's my duty to see that you're delivered safe and sound."

"Delivered? To whom?"

The lieutenant shook his head. "That I can't say."

"Can't, or won't?"

"Neither."

"Can you tell me who brought me aboard, then?"

"You ask a lot of questions. If the captain wants you to know that, he'll tell you."

"Good. Take me to him, then."

"When he wants to see you, he'll send for you."

"And what am I to do in the meanwhile?" he demanded.

The lieutenant regarded him coolly as he poured himself another shot of rum. "Well, if I was you," he said, "I'd work on my manners."

Creighton couldn't escape this room by climbing out the window. For one thing, the window was too small. For another, there was nothing beyond it but water—and possibly a few sharks. So he continued to lie helpless on the bunk, silently seething.

Twice a day the lieutenant, whose name was Hervey Hale, brought him a pewter dish of food—at least that was what Hale called it. Creighton called it slop. He made it clear that he was accustomed to better fare than boiled beef and bread.

"At least it's fresh," Hale said. "Wait until we've been at sea a fortnight or so. Then it'll be beans and salt junk and lobscouse."

"*Lobscouse?* It sounds dreadful."

Hale nodded grimly. "It is. It's dried potato slices, cooked to the consistency of leather."

After two days of sulking, Creighton was escorted at last to the captain's quarters. Captain Pierce was a thin, almost gaunt man with a long white scar across his forehead. His right coat sleeve, absent an arm, was folded up and pinned at the shoulder. "Ah, Mr. Brown," he said. "Come in."

"Do you need me to stand by, sir?" asked Lieutenant Hale.

"No, thank you. I believe I can handle him." The captain closed the door of the cabin and gestured to an upholstered chair. "Sit down, please."

Creighton was taken off guard by the man's cordial manner. Then the indignation that had been fermenting inside him burst forth. "I don't want to sit down! I want to know why I'm here, and what you're going to do about it!"

The captain's reaction threw him off balance again. The man smiled.

"I'm sorry, did I say something amusing?" Creighton asked.

"No. Just predictable." The captain took a seat at his desk.

"Predictable?"

"Yes. They told me you'd be . . . difficult."

"There it is again! *They!* What *they* are we talking about?"

The captain ran a finger thoughtfully along the scar on his forehead. "I suppose you'll learn sooner or later, anyway. You were brought aboard by Sir Edward Lyndon."

"Lyndon?" Creighton said incredulously. Feeling suddenly weak, he sank down into the chair.

"You know him, I gather."

"Of course. He's a . . . a *friend* of my mother's, I suppose you'd say, though I'm sure he considers himself more than that—a suitor, no doubt, even though my mother is still in mourning for my father. So, this was his doing?"

Captain Pierce nodded. "This is Sir Edward's ship, the *Amity*."

Creighton put his head in his hands. "I don't understand. Why would he— I—I know well enough that he dislikes me, and I'm certain he's aware that I disapprove of him and of his . . . attentions to my mother. But what can he possibly hope to gain from shipping me off like this? Surely he realizes that if my mother hears of it, she'll have nothing further to do with him." The captain made no reply. Creighton raised his head. "Did he tell you where you were to deliver me?"

The captain looked uncomfortable. "No. Not exactly." With his sole hand he reached inside his coat and drew out a folded paper. "He gave me this, with instructions to pass it on to you sometime before we reach the Colonies. I thought that sooner would be better." He handed the paper to Creighton.

On the back, in familiar handwriting, was a name and address: *Colonel Hugh Gower, The State House, Charles Town, South Carolina Colony.* The blob of red sealing wax had been impressed with a design he had seen a hundred times—a rose—and the paper itself smelled faintly of rose petals.

Ignoring the fact that the letter was not addressed to him, Creighton broke the seal and unfolded the paper. The message within was brief:

My Dear Brother,

Ever since Harry's death, our son Creighton has become more and more difficult to manage. I will not give a detailed account of the troubles he has caused; as I recall, you are intimately acquainted with the sorts of mischief of which a boy this age is capable.

I will only say that I can no longer control him, and that my attempts to do so have driven me to distraction. I am hoping that you will see fit to take him for a time. He is not a bad boy, truly. Under your guidance, and away from the influence of those knaves he calls friends, I believe he may make something of himself yet.

I know that I am asking a good deal of you, that you have many other pressing duties and concerns, but I also know that you are not insensible of the fact that you are, in some measure, responsible for the helpless circumstances in which I find myself, and may welcome this as an opportunity to satisfy your conscience.

With gratitude, I am

Yr. affec. sister,
Charlotte

Dazed, Creighton let the letter fall from his grasp and flutter to the floor. "My God," he groaned, "I've been exiled to the Wilderness."

———◆◆◆———

Chapter THREE

*F*or several days afterward, Creighton did little but lie in his bunk and brood upon his fate. He read and reread his mother's letter, half convinced that he had misunderstood its message, or had missed something. But the message was clear—she wanted to be rid of him.

Each time he unfolded the paper, the faint fragrance of rose petals sent an almost nauseating wave of homesickness washing over him. At night he fancied he could sense the smell seeping from beneath his pillow. Finally, he ripped the paper to shreds and flung the pieces from the window of the cabin. But the wind was against him, and half the bits blew back in his face. Furious, he gathered them up and cast them out again, and yet again, in a sort of frenzy, sobbing "Get out! Get out! I don't *want* you!" until at last he had consigned every scrap of paper to the waves.

In his worst moments of despair, he even cursed his father, for dying and leaving him to be raised by a mother who was capable of giving him neither understanding nor discipline. Like an inmate of a prison, Creighton kept track of the slowly passing days by scratching marks on the wall of the cabin above his bunk—until Hervey Hale noticed and ordered him to stop. Creighton glared at him. "I don't have to take orders from you. I'm not a Marine."

"No, but this is my quarters and I'll thank you not to destroy it."

Creighton glanced about the room, which, despite the fact that the lieutenant seemed to have very few worldly possessions, somehow contrived to look cluttered and untidy. "As if it matters," he muttered.

"I'm sure it's not as grand as what you're used to," Hale replied, unperturbed, "but it suits me."

Creighton eyed the man's equally untidy uniform, which at the moment sported a sprinkling of shredded tobacco down the front. "There's no question about that."

The lieutenant shrugged. "If there's one thing life in the military has taught me—and it has taught me a good many things—"

"Clearly neatness is not one of them."

Hale ignored him. "If there's one thing it's taught me, it is that you can't judge a man by his appearance, nor by his speech. The only thing that counts is what he does."

"And what have *you* done lately?" Creighton asked archly.

Hale regarded him soberly for a moment, and Creighton saw something in the gaze that made him wonder if perhaps he had underestimated the man. The lieutenant's knowing look somehow conveyed the feeling that, if he chose, he could tell some tales Creighton might not care to hear, tales that dealt with a side of life from which Creighton had so far been sheltered.

But Hale apparently did not choose to. Instead he scratched his nose and said dryly, "Well, I've put up with you, and that's a test of any man's mettle."

Creighton could not suppress a bit of a smile. "How much longer do we have to put up with each other, then?"

"Four to six weeks, most likely, depending."

"On what?"

"On whether or not the winds favor us, and whether or not there's any trouble."

"Trouble? What sort?"

Hale shrugged. "Could be bad weather. Could be pirates."

"Pirates?"

"They call themselves privateers, just as though we were still at war, but they're nothing more nor less than pirates. We haven't run afoul of any the last few trips, but two years ago they came near to sinking this very vessel." He leaned back in his bunk and gazed out the window, as though looking for pirates on the horizon.

Creighton bent forward eagerly. Suddenly the man's conversation did not seem so dull. "What happened?"

"She was an American ship, the *Revenge,* but she was showing British colors. She overtook us off Cuba. Her captain steered across our course and jammed her bowsprit up among our forward rigging so we were all tangled together. We traded cannon fire and musket fire for a time, with us giving as good as we got. I knew we had to cut our-selves loose somehow, but going aloft was like stepping into the fiery furnace.

"The captain has never been one to ask of another what he won't do himself. So he scrambled up the ropes and commenced hacking at the tangled rigging with his saber. He got us free, all right, but not before a ball from the *Revenge* shattered his arm."

Creighton had not realized he was holding his breath until he let it out in a long sigh. "Do you suppose there's any chance we'll encounter pirates this trip?" he asked hopefully. When he was younger, his greatest ambition had been to join, or better yet lead, a band of pirates.

Hale turned from the window with a fierce expression that somehow resembled a smile. "I hope so," he said.

The following day, Creighton discovered something else about Lieutenant Hale—the man was a crack cardplayer. Predictably, the only deck he owned was dog-eared and grease-stained, but Creighton consented to join him in a game of brag. By the time they put in at the Azores to take on fresh fruit and water, he had schooled Creighton in the fine points not only of brag but of commerce and quadrille and basset.

Since Creighton had no money, the currency they used for betting was grains of rice; they had tried using dried peas, but in a heavy sea the little green spheres were con-stantly rolling off the edge of the table.

During their brief stopover in the Azores, Creighton was again confined to the cabin so he wouldn't be tempted to escape. He looked longingly at the vessels anchored nearby and wondered which of them were bound for the British Isles. Had the window been a bit larger, he might have plunged into the water and swum to one of the other ships. He considered shouting for help out the window, but the memory of how the cloth gag had felt in his mouth made him reconsider.

Besides, he had another strategy in mind. If his mother had hoped that unloading him upon his uncle would somehow set him on the straight and narrow path, she would be sorely disappointed. Creighton had no intention of reforming, and every intention of making himself so willful, unmanageable, and obnoxious that the colonel would be ready to ship him back to England within a week.

Like Hale, Captain Pierce seemed to welcome the prospect of a pirate attack, as a chance to avenge himself. But the chance never came. They sailed into Charles Town unmolested. Creighton, who expected living conditions in America to be primitive at best, was unprepared for the sight that met his eyes. The broad inlet that served as a harbor was positively crowded with craft of all sizes and descriptions, from small fishing smacks and spider catchers to barges laden with indigo and rice to huge square riggers. Creighton estimated they shared the anchorage with at least two hundred vessels, not counting the swarm of rowboats that ferried constantly between the ships and the shore.

A dinghy was lowered over the side of the *Amity* and a small party that included the captain, the sailing master,

Lieutenant Hale, and Creighton set off toward a long wooden dock that projected into the bay.

Because the city was situated on a point of land bounded by two rivers, it had an extensive waterfront. It was lined with warehouses, and every inch of it teemed with activity. They disembarked near a vast two-story structure Captain Pierce referred to as the Exchange. The captain extended his hand to Creighton, who shook it awkwardly with his own left hand. "I hope you'll find the New World to your liking."

"I don't expect to," Creighton replied. "Nor do I expect it will like me very much." He glanced about uncertainly. "Where might I look for my uncle?"

"At the State House. I believe he is Governor Campbell's military aide. Lieutenant Hale will escort you there."

Creighton had expected to find narrow dirt streets and unimposing clapboard houses. Instead, the streets were broad and paved with stone—in fact, Lieutenant Hale informed him, it was English stone, brought over in the holds of ships as ballast. The homes were as grand as anything in Bristol, constructed of gray-brown bricks, with tile roofs. Some were more in the nature of mansions, their landscaped grounds surrounded by high brick walls with wrought-iron gates. Nearly all the houses had deep, shady verandas on all four sides. The porches looked cool and welcoming, for even in April the air here was uncomfortably warm.

His uncle's quarters, within the thick walls of the State House, were cool enough, but there was nothing welcoming about them. A pinched-faced civilian clerk was perched at a writing desk, sharpening the tip of a quill with a small folding knife. When Creighton and the lieutenant entered, the clerk didn't even bother to glance their way, but bent over his ledger intently, like a surgeon about to operate. After a moment's wait, Hale stepped forward and laid a thick arm on the edge of the man's desk. "You want to tell me where we can find Colonel Gower," he said, and it was not a question.

The clerk looked Hale up and down as though the lieutenant were a beggar come to ask for a handout. "Who wants to know?"

"His nephew," Hale replied.

The clerk raised his eyebrows. "*You're* his nephew?"

"Of course not, you fool. *He* is."

The clerk gave Creighton the same sort of supercilious look. "The colonel is not in," he said at last.

"Well, where *is* he?"

The clerk nodded toward a window that looked out onto the street. "At the guardhouse."

Creighton moved to the window. In front of the building across the way, several ranks of soldiers stood at attention, facing a wooden post to which another soldier, stripped to the waist, was tied by the wrists. A burly sergeant stepped forward and drew some object from a leather pouch. When he shook it, a number of strands dangled free, and Creighton realized it was a cat-o'-nine-tails. As he watched, with the same sort of horrid fascination the hanging of Tom Corbett had inspired, the sergeant raised the whip and laid it across the naked torso of the man at the post. The victim arched his back and bit his lip, but did not cry out—at least not at the first half-dozen blows.

By the tenth—Creighton found he was counting the strokes under his breath—the man was bellowing with pain, and his back was a latticework of red welts, some of them oozing blood. By fifteen, the soldier's knees had buckled, and all that kept him upright were the thongs that bound him to the post.

When the count reached twenty, the man was cut loose and dragged into the guardhouse. A voice called "Dismissed!" and the ranks of soldiers began to break up. Only then did Creighton notice the solitary figure who stood watching from several paces away. In one hand he grasped a rolled-up paper, which he was smacking rhythmically into the palm of the other hand, as though mentally giving the prisoner several more lashes. Though the man did not look at all familiar to Creighton, he had no doubt that it was his uncle.

The colonel had the same sort of stocky build as Hale, but there the resemblance ended. There was nothing untidy about the colonel. His red coat and his fawn-colored knee breeches and waistcoat were well tailored and neatly pressed. His shirtfront lacked the ruffled lace favored by officers back home, but its linen was spotless, and his boots, though worn, were newly polished.

Though Gower had visited his sister's family a few times before being assigned to duty in the Colonies, Creighton had been very young; the only detail he had remembered about his uncle was a powdered wig, which had come off when Creighton tugged at it, frightening the boy badly. Apparently wigs were not in fashion in America, for the colonel no longer wore one. His dark hair—threaded with gray even though he could be no more than forty—was worn long and tied at the nape of the neck with a plain black ribbon. Like most military men, he had no beard or mustache, but his side-whiskers extended several inches below his cheekbones.

Once the soldiers had dispersed, he turned and started toward the State House, slapping the rolled paper absently against his thigh as he walked. His gaze went to the window, and he seemed for the first time to catch sight of Creighton standing there. He paused momentarily, looking slightly puzzled, or perhaps wary. It was difficult to gauge his expression; his eyes were so narrow and so deep-set that Creighton could read nothing in them. He could not even tell whether or not they were green, like his mother's eyes.

The only obvious trait Hugh Gower shared with his sister was a long and slightly irregular nose, with which he seemed to be sniffing the air, like a wolf searching for a scent that would tell him whether he faced a friend or a foe.

Creighton stared back at the colonel, wondering the same thing. Now that the man was nearer, the purpose of the long side-whiskers became clear: to help conceal the deep pockmarks that disfigured the colonel's face—the familiar battle scars borne by the survivors of the smallpox.

Creighton turned from the window. A moment later his uncle strode into the room, glancing from Hale to Creighton and back again. "Are these gentlemen here to see me?" he asked the clerk.

Before the man could reply, Hervey Hale stepped up and saluted. "Lieutenant Hale, sir, of the schooner *Amity*. I've brought you your nephew."

The colonel's eyes narrowed even further. "My nephew, is it?" He approached Creighton, surveying him critically, as he might a raw recruit.

"Creighton," the boy reminded him. "Major Harry Brown's son."

"I'm aware of that." Colonel Gower examined him further. "You don't resemble your father at all. You're more like your mother. She sent you to me, no doubt. She's complained in her letters about your . . . undisciplined behavior. I suppose she thought I'd be the one to shape you up."

"No. In fact, I came of my own accord." As was often the case with his lies, Creighton hadn't consciously planned this one. It had simply come forth, as it were, of its own accord. But he liked the sound of it; certainly it was more comfortable than the truth. And it might prove useful. If his uncle believed that coming here had been Creighton's own idea, he might be more inclined to let his nephew go home when it became obvious—as it would—that Creighton was not cut out for life in the Colonies.

He heard Lieutenant Hale clear his throat, and he tensed, afraid the man would reveal that Creighton had, in fact, been abducted. "If you have no further need of me," said the gruff voice, "I'll report back to my ship."

"Yes, all right. Thank you for seeing my nephew here safely." The colonel drew out his purse. "Is there anything owing for his passage?"

"No, sir."

"Here's something for your trouble, then." He tossed a half crown to the lieutenant. As Hale turned to go, he gave Creighton a quizzical, warning glance that said, *I hope you know what you're doing, lad.*

Creighton felt a rush of relief, knowing that Hale wouldn't betray him. Then he tensed again as Colonel Gower called, "One moment, Lieutenant."

Hale turned back. "Sir?"

"Where is your ship bound from here?"

"To Florida, to trade for cypress and cedar, then to Barbados, then home."

The colonel nodded thoughtfully. "And when do you sail?"

"Tomorrow or the day after, most likely."

Gower nodded again. "Very well. That's all."

The colonel showed Creighton into his chambers. They were furnished in a sparse and Spartan fashion, as though Gower had little use for comfort or elegance, or as though he did not expect to be here long. His sitting room hardly deserved the name; there was not much to sit on, only a couple of uncomfortable-looking ladder-back chairs. Between the chairs was a small tea table. There was also a larger table containing a few papers, a candle, and a silver inkwell. On the mantelpiece over the fireplace sat a clock, a mug, a pipe, a wooden humidor, and a steel tinderbox. The door to the bedchamber was ajar, revealing a simple bedstead with an ironbound war trunk at the foot.

There was only one window in the sitting room, and it faced the street. Feeling ill at ease in the wolf's lair, Creighton strolled to the window and gazed out at the guardhouse. The yard before it was empty now, except for the blood-spattered post. "What was the whipping for?" he asked.

"What?" The colonel's tone suggested that he was not accustomed to being questioned.

"The whipping. Was that man a deserter?"

"No." Gower held out the paper he had been carrying. "A copy of this was found in his possession."

Creighton glanced at the paper. It was a four-sided broadsheet, like those hawked by vendors at executions and other public gatherings. The heading on the front page read THE LIBERTY TREE. "A newspaper?"

"A *subversive* newspaper, circulated by a group calling themselves the Sons of Liberty."

"Rebels? Here in Carolina?"

"We don't know where it's printed, but somehow it has worked its way into all the Colonies, like a noxious weed that spreads its tendrils no matter how often you cut them back."

"It must be dangerous stuff," Creighton said sarcastically, "if you can get twenty lashes just for reading a copy."

Gower gave him an irritable glance. "Harsh discipline helps to assure that others don't make the same mistake."

He tossed the paper onto the table. "That's something your father failed to understand."

"My father? What do you mean?"

"I mean that he let his judgment be impaired by his compassion." Before Creighton could ask him to explain, he went on. "I suppose you came here for the same reason your father did."

"And what reason is that?"

"Why, to get away from my sister."

Creighton frowned, half-puzzled, half-offended. "I don't believe that was my father's reason. I believe he wanted to serve in the Colonies because it afforded more opportunity for advancement."

The colonel laughed humorlessly. "I expect that any desire for advancement was more on your mother's part than your father's. Harry was not an ambitious sort. You can be sure that he would not have advanced as far as he did had it not been for my influence."

"You mean . . . my father was assigned here, to Carolina, on your recommendation?"

"He was."

"So that's what my mother meant when she said you were partly responsible for his . . . for his fate."

Gower scowled at him. "She said that? The ungrateful woman! She asked me to find a good position for him, and I did. She said nothing about keeping him safe. In any case, Carolina was as safe at the time as any place in the Colonies—far safer than New York or Boston, certainly."

"How . . . how did he come to be killed, then?"

The colonel's scowl deepened. "I don't know all the particulars. What does it matter, in any case? Dead is dead."

Though his uncle's callousness irked him, Creighton managed to sound reasonably polite. "May I at least see his grave?"

"It's a good distance from here. There won't be time."

"Well, not today, perhaps, but surely—"

"We'll see," Gower said impatiently, then turned toward the doorway and shouted, "Norris!"

A moment later the pinched-faced clerk appeared. "Sir?"

"Go and tell them to prepare an extra place for tea."

"Yes, sir." The clerk disappeared again.

"I thought they'd given up the practice of drinking tea here in America," Creighton said.

"They have, by and large, in favor of *coffee.*" He pronounced the word with obvious distaste. "However, I have no intention of giving it up." He waved a hand dismissively, as though to convey that he had had enough of small talk and meant to get down to business. "So. If you are not here to escape my sister, what is your purpose?"

"I wanted to see something more of the world than just England," Creighton lied blithely. "My mother says that a gentleman should be well traveled and well informed."

"Does she? And how do you find Carolina so far?"

"It seems pleasant enough," Creighton said cautiously, not wanting to give the impression that he might actually be willing to stay.

"Good. Of course it doesn't much matter what you think of it, since you won't be staying long."

"Not be staying . . . ? You mean . . . you're sending me home?" he said hopefully.

His uncle turned a suspicious look upon him. "You sound as though you welcome the prospect. Yet you just told me that coming here was your own idea."

They were interrupted by the arrival of a serving maid, who curtsied and then swiftly and silently placed a china pot and cups on the tea table, along with a plate of small, frosted cakes. Ordinarily Creighton would have attacked the cakes at once, but just now his appetite was dulled by an uneasy feeling in his gut.

When the maid was gone, he said, "It was my idea to come here. I only wondered what you meant, about my not staying long."

The colonel took his time in replying. He poured tea for them both, then sipped at his. "I mean," he said, at last, "that His Majesty has seen fit to appoint me lieutenant governor of West Florida. We depart in a day or two."

Chapter FOUR

For several moments Creighton was too dazed by this revelation to speak. He could almost have resigned himself to six months or even a year in Charles Town. But *Florida*?

It could hardly even be called a colony. England had won it from Spain only ten or fifteen years before. But perhaps *won* was not the proper term. That implied the transfer of something valuable, whereas, from everything Creighton had heard or read in school, Florida was one large sweltering swamp, filled with alligators, mosquitoes, dire diseases, wild Indians, and sand bogs that swallowed a man without a trace.

Creighton shook his head and gave a strained laugh. "No, no. I didn't bargain on Florida when I came here."

"Life is seldom what one bargained for. Besides, it seems to me that you have little choice in the matter. You can hardly stay behind in Charles Town. You know no one here. You have no means of supporting yourself."

"I could return to England," Creighton suggested.

"If you had the price of passage. But I doubt that you do. In fact, I doubt that you had the money to pay for your trip here. I suspect that Sir Edward Lyndon provided your passage, as a favor to my sister."

"What makes you think that?" Creighton said, doing his best to sound indignant.

The colonel's narrow eyes regarded him reprovingly over the rim of his teacup. "Whatever else my sister may have said about me, I'm fairly certain she did not characterize me as a fool."

"No."

"Then do not behave as though I were one!" He set his cup down so forcefully that Creighton flinched. "In any case, it doesn't matter how or why you came. Now that you are here, I am responsible for you. That means you will go where I go, and you will do as I say."

As much as he hated to admit it, his uncle was right. Creighton was smart enough to find a way out of going to Florida; all he'd have to do was hide out somewhere when the ship was due to sail. But he was also smart enough to know that he couldn't hope to manage here on his own. He'd never had to fend for himself before, and he certainly wasn't about to start now, in an unfamiliar land.

He could still try to make himself so unbearable that his uncle would beg him to go home. But the more he saw of the man, the more unlikely that plan seemed. Gower was clearly a far tougher nut than Creighton's mother had been. Instead of being driven to distraction, as his mother had put it, the colonel might be driven to something more drastic, such as discipline—and Creighton had seen an example of his brand of discipline.

He tried to console himself with the thought that perhaps, like Carolina, Florida would not be as abysmal as he imagined. That hope was dashed when his uncle's clerk revealed, with obvious relish, the reason why a new lieutenant governor was wanted: The conditions of life in the colony had driven the old one mad, and he'd put a bullet through his brain.

After two days of desperate pondering, Creighton came up with a new plan: He would meekly accompany his uncle to Florida. But when the *Amity* set sail for Barbados and the return trip to England, he would be aboard her, concealed belowdecks somewhere.

The following day they boarded the ship for the voyage to Pensacola, the capital city—if it could be called that—of West Florida. Captain Pierce greeted Creighton like an old friend and installed him and his uncle in a cabin that was far more spacious and neat than the one Creighton had shared with Hervey Hale.

Though Creighton cringed at the prospect of being in such close quarters with his uncle, he reminded himself that it would be for only a short while—no more than a week, according to Captain Pierce. To Creighton's relief, Gower spent much of his time in the company of the captain—swapping war stories, no doubt. Despite a sizable window, the cabin was stifling, and Creighton took to wandering about the ship for hours on end, getting in the way of sailors who were scouring the decks with holystones or pulling at the haul-yards, and stumbling over others who were mending sail or picking oakum.

When Creighton was younger, his father had often taken him on board Sir Robert's merchant vessels. Though Creighton had no real fondness for his grandfather, he would gladly have accompanied his father anywhere. It was a mystery to him how Harry Brown could have grown up to be so easygoing and good-humored when he had been raised by such a bossy, crotchety old man. Sir Robert seemed to disapprove most of the very things that most appealed to Creighton. One of these things was to scramble up the standing rigging to the crow's nest, sixty feet above the deck, where he launched gobbets of spittle deck-ward while Sir Robert ordered him, in vain, to come down.

Now, bored with the sameness of shipboard life and hoping for a glimpse of land, Creighton heaved himself up onto the shrouds that supported the mainmast and began to climb the ladderlike ratlines. "Here, you daft lad!" called a sailor with an unruly mass of sun-bleached blond hair. "Get down from there before you break your fool neck!" Creighton heeded him no more than he had ever heeded his grandfather.

"Let him kill himself, then," he heard another sailor say. " 'Twill be no great loss." Creighton considered sending a wad of spit onto the man's shaved head, but concluded that it would not be the gentlemanly thing to do.

Though the captain had said they were rounding the cape of Florida, Creighton could sight no land in any direction. But there was a breath of wind that gave him temporary relief from the subtropical heat. Steamy days like this were unknown in Bristol, even at the height of summer. Creighton removed his coat, spread his arms, and let the sluggish breeze ruffle his linen shirt.

According to sailing superstition, to whistle while a ship was under way was to invite a gale. Creighton closed his eyes and began to whistle softly, wishing that the wind would rise into a gale strong enough to sweep him from the crow's nest and carry him home.

When he opened his eyes again, an irregular dark spot on the horizon lay directly in his line of vision. Shading his face from the sun with one hand and grasping a shroud with the other, he stared at the spot until his eyes watered. He had always prided himself on his keen eyesight; it would be a feather in his cap if he was the first person aboard to catch sight of landfall. But he wasn't certain that it was land. As the distance between them diminished, he was able to make out a hull and three masts. Cupping a hand over his mouth, he called toward the deck below, "Ahoy! A sail!"

The towheaded gob who had chastised him for climbing called back, "Where?"

"Off the larboard bow!"

Half a dozen men rushed to the larboard rail. Creighton descended the ratlines in time to hear one of them say, "She's rigged fore-and-aft, not square."

The boatswain joined them at the rail. "Looks like a snow."

Creighton knew most types of vessels, but this was one he hadn't heard of. "What's a snow?"

"It's these little white flakes that fall out o' the sky," said the blond-haired man.

The boatswain grinned and shook his head. "Never mind him. A snow is similar to a schooner, but faster and more maneuverable. You don't see them often back home, but they're a favorite here in the Colonies—particularly among privateers." He turned to the blond man. "Has anyone alerted the captain?"

"Aye. He's having a look at it through his spyglass, I'll wager."

"Do you think it's a privateer?" Creighton asked breathlessly.

The boatswain shrugged. "No way to tell, at this range."

Creighton hurried aft to the quarterdeck. Captain Pierce was surveying the vessel through the lens of a collapsible brass telescope. Colonel Gower stood next to him, his long nose seemingly searching the breeze for a scent from the strange ship. "Can you make out her colors?" the colonel asked.

"She's flying the Union Jack," the captain said. "For what that's worth. So was the *Revenge*—right up until the moment she rammed into my ship."

"If it is a privateer," said Creighton, "can we outrun her?"

"I'm afraid not. They're running with the wind; we're against it. By the time we could come about, they'd be on top of us. Chances are she's only a trader, headed for the Indies. I wish I could get a look at the figurehead; that might tell me something. But the jib is obscuring it. There's no name on the bow, either." He handed the telescope to Colonel Gower.

Lieutenant Hale approached, nodded to Creighton, and saluted the captain. "Orders, sir?"

"Arm your men and station yourselves behind the larboard gunwales, but stay out of sight. No firing unless I order it. Tell the gunners to load the cannon and stand by, but not to open the gun ports. If she is a merchant ship, we don't want her crew to think that *we're* attacking *them.*"

"Aye, sir." The lieutenant scurried back down the steps to the main deck.

"Any sign that they're preparing for hostilities, Colonel?" Captain Pierce asked.

"None. And none of their gun ports are open."

Creighton's gaze was drawn to the top of the snow's mainmast. "They're lowering the flag and hoisting another—No, wait. It's still the British colors, but wrong side up."

"A signal of distress," the captain said. "Again, for what it's worth."

Creighton glanced at him in surprise. "Surely even a privateer would not be so treacherous as to fly a fake distress signal?"

Colonel Gower gave an unpleasant laugh. "You're assuming that we're dealing with honorable men. Expecting honor from an American is like expecting milk from a snake."

The snow was so near now that Creighton could discern individual figures lining the rail, waving to them—figures with long hair and dresses. "There are women aboard!"

Captain Pierce took the telescope and trained it on the ship. "You're right." He called to the first mate, "Shiver the sails!" and to the sailing master at the helm, "Hard alee!" The snow slackened her canvas as well, and the two vessels continued to coast until they were abreast of each other. One of the women aboard the snow was leaning out over the rail, calling something to them, but the wind

46

swept her words away. A moment later it also swept away her long tresses.

"The devil take me!" cried the captain. "They've tricked us!" He strode to the rail that overlooked the main deck. "It's a ruse, gentlemen! Prepare to—" His command was cut off by an ear-numbing roar, like a peal of thunder, but ten times louder. In the same instant there came a sickening splintering sound, and suddenly the air was filled with flying bits of wood and metal.

Creighton fell to his knees, his arms covering his head, while objects rained down around him. Something struck him in the small of the back, driving him facedown on the deck. There followed a moment of silence so profound that he feared his eardrums had been burst by the blast. Then, to his bewilderment, he heard voices cheering and clamoring. Groaning, Creighton rose to his knees, throwing off whatever object had struck him, and stared at the snow.

Its entire crew were lined up along the rail, shouting and waving weapons above their heads in triumph. At the base of the gunwales where a moment before there had appeared to be a row of closed gun ports, there was now a series of gaping holes, fringed with flapping streamers of canvas. It took a second or two for the truth to sink into Creighton's dazed mind: The ports had not been closed at all, only covered over with squares of sailcloth, painted to resemble wood. The shot from the snow's cannon had ripped effortlessly through them and then through the *Amity*'s hull and rigging.

As the cheers from the other ship died down, Creighton became aware of other voices, crying for help or moaning in pain. He looked out over the main deck. It was the scene of the most incredible chaos and carnage. Broken spars, ragged chunks of sailcloth, and rigging torn asunder were strewn everywhere. Tangled in the debris were bodies, some writhing in agony, some struggling to rise, others as still as death.

What remained of Lieutenant Hale's Marines were crouched behind what remained of the gunwales, loading and firing their muskets methodically, mechanically, like marionettes with no will of their own. A handful of other crewmen, most of them bleeding from superficial wounds, were wrestling the *Amity*'s cannon into position for an answering volley.

Still on his knees, Creighton turned to survey the quarterdeck and saw for the first time the crumpled form beside him. Captain Pierce lay sprawled on his back, his eyes wide open, as though in astonishment. A long, jagged shard of oak from the shattered mainmast protruded from the base of his neck.

A hand seized Creighton's arm. He jerked free and spun about, expecting to see a pirate with a raised cutlass towering over him. Colonel Gower snatched Creighton's coat sleeve again. "Come with me!"

"What about the captain?"

"He's done for! Come!"

"They need our help here!" Creighton protested.

"This is more important." The colonel ushered him into their cabin, slammed the door, and bolted it. Then he produced a key from his waistcoat pocket and bent over his war chest. "Do you know how to strike a fire?"

"A fire?"

"Yes, yes." His uncle dug the tinderbox from the chest and held it out.

Creighton shook his head. "I never had to. At home, the servants always—"

"You're even more useless than I thought!" the colonel growled. He snatched his leather diplomatic pouch from the chest and thrust it into Creighton's hands. "You can at least empty that out, I hope."

"Of course. But where—"

"On the floor!" The ship gave a nauseating lurch, pitching them both off balance. "They're pulling us in with grappling hooks. Be quick now! They'll be boarding us soon."

Creighton unbuckled the pouch and upended it, dumping out its contents, a sheaf of official papers. "What are you going to do?"

"Burn them, of course. We can't let them fall into enemy hands." The colonel crouched down and began striking the flint against the steel cover of the box. Sparks rained down on the linen scrapings inside the box. "Now listen to me," he went on, his words punctuated by the click of flint against steel. "Whatever happens, you're not to let anyone know you're my nephew."

"Why not?"

"If you do, they'll try to obtain a ransom for you. From this moment, you are my bound boy, nothing more. Understood?"

"But won't they—"

His uncle glared at him. "No *questions,* boy! Just do as I say!" The flint clashed fiercely against the tinderbox. At the same moment something heavy pounded against the door of the cabin and a harsh voice shouted, "Open at once!"

The tinder had begun to smolder. When Colonel Gower laid it on the pile of papers and blew gently on it, it burst into flame. As the blaze grew, the colonel fed the papers to it, one by one, ignoring the insistent pounding at the door.

Before the documents were quite consumed by the flames, the bolt gave way. The door flew open, crashing against the wall, and the largest man Creighton had ever seen burst inside—or rather *ducked* inside, since he was nearly a foot taller than the doorframe. Creighton had heard it said that everything in America was on a larger scale than in England, but he had never expected Yankeys to be a race of giants.

A second man entered the room then, and he was of normal size, or even a bit less. But his swarthy complexion and hawklike features, and the wild look in his eyes, made him nearly as intimidating as the giant. Each of the men bore a cutlass in one hand and a boarding pistol equipped with a bayonet in the other.

At their entrance, Colonel Gower had sprung to his feet

and drawn his saber. The short American leveled his pistol at the colonel's chest. "It doesn't matter to me, sir, whether I shoot you or not," he said. "But I daresay it will matter to you."

━━━◆✦◆━━━

Chapter FIVE

*W*ithout even waiting for the colonel to lower his weapon, the man pushed Gower aside with the edge of the bayonet and stamped out the burning pile of papers. "Take the man's weapon, Peter, and bind his hands." He turned to Creighton. "What about you? Do you mean to give us any trouble?"

Creighton spread his arms. "I've no weapon."

As the colonel's hands were tied behind him, he protested, "This is an outrage! I am an officer in His Majesty's army!"

"You are also a prisoner," said the short man.

"By whose orders?"

"Mine." The man bowed, in a fashion that seemed to hold a touch of mockery. "Benedict Arnold, sir, general of the Continental Army, at your service." He certainly looked nothing like a general, or any sort of officer. But, Creighton had to admit, neither did he fit the popular image of a pirate. In fact, his modest but fashionable brown breeches and russet coat gave him the appearance of a prosperous merchant.

The colonel laughed derisively. "There is no Continental Army. We defeated it."

"Ah, but we never surrendered, and we signed no treaty."

"Treaties are for wars. Your pitiful campaign was a rebellion, nothing more."

The American's face went tight. Creighton feared for a moment he might shoot the colonel, or impale him. But he answered only with words. "You know, that's one of the things we can't abide about you Brits—your damned arrogance."

Arnold crouched to examine the pile of charred papers, keeping his right leg out straight beside him, as though it pained him to bend it. "It's a pity we didn't force the door a minute sooner. These might have proven to be informative." He tossed the blackened pieces aside, then picked up the diplomatic pouch and peered inside. "Hello. What have we here?" He drew out a sheet of paper that had somehow stuck inside the pouch.

Creighton glanced guiltily at his uncle, whose expression was a mixture of disbelief and disgust. Without speaking a word, he clearly conveyed how low was his opinion of his nephew's worth.

Arnold's thick black eyebrows rose. "A letter to the governor of West Florida, from the governor of South Carolina. It appears that our prisoner is to be the colony's new lieutenant governor. Or *was* to be, should I say?"

"Gad!" exclaimed the giant. "He should fetch us a pretty price."

Arnold nodded thoughtfully, his gaze fixed on the colonel's face, as though he were trying recall where he had seen it before. "Colonel Gower, is it? I know that name. You were at Quebec, were you not?"

"I was. My men defended the water gate."

"Then it's you I have to thank for this memorable souvenir of my visit to Canada." The American got awkwardly to his feet, one hand pressing on the thigh of his injured leg.

"It was a visit for which your men paid dearly, I believe," said the colonel. "Still, we captured far more than we killed. I must say, that surprised me, in view of the little mottoes that were pinned to the caps of those who surrendered: *Liberty or Death.* Yet when it came down to it, most of them chose to live, even in captivity."

Arnold raised his cutlass and placed the point against the top button of the colonel's coat. "And which do you choose, sir? Life in captivity? Or death?"

Colonel Gower did not flinch. "If you mean to hold me for ransom, you're wasting your time. My government will not negotiate with brigands."

"Oh, we had no intention of asking for a ransom. We will demand an exchange. And since I've often heard it said that one of your soldiers is worth at least three of ours, they'll no doubt agree to give us three American officers in exchange for you."

"What about that one?" the giant named Peter said, pointing his sword at Creighton.

The warning look his uncle sent in his direction was every bit as sharp. "No one would give a farthing for me," Creighton said. "I'm only a servant." He knew well enough that his speech sounded nothing like a servant's; if it did, all his years of elocution lessons would have been wasted. But he was just as certain that these uncultured Yankeys would not know the difference.

"What sort of servant?" Peter asked. "Hired or bound?"

"Bound."

The man nodded sympathetically. "I know how that works. All they do is pay your passage, and you're theirs for seven years. 'Tis not much different from being a slave."

Now that Creighton had a better look at him, he realized that the giant was probably only a year or two older than he was. His voice was unexpectedly high, as though it had not yet matured, and his manner of speaking, which was deliberate and earnest, with a trace of a lisp, made him sound a trifle slow-witted.

The other American's curt, intense manner contrasted as sharply with the giant's as did his size. When he spoke, it was as though every word were a command. "Well," he said, "your indenture will be an unexpectedly short one. We Patriots are not in the habit of keeping slaves." He stared at the colonel a moment, as if considering what to do with him. "Lock our prisoner in the captain's cabin. It looks as though the captain will no longer be needing it."

"It's not necessary to confine me," Colonel Gower assured him. "I am willing to give my word as an officer and a gentleman that I will not attempt to escape."

"You may be willing to give your word," said Arnold. "But I am not willing to take it." He beckoned to Creighton. "You may come with me." Creighton hesitated and gave a guarded glance at his uncle. The colonel made a slight sideways motion with his head, as if to say, *Go with him.*

Most of the privateers were aboard the *Amity* now. Judging from their lack of injuries, they had taken the ship without much of a fight. The dozen or so British sailors and Marines who had come through relatively unscathed—Creighton was relieved to see Lieutenant Hale among them—were being herded together and their legs shackled with chains. Those who had been sorely wounded were being bandaged and given drinks of rum by the Americans. The dead were being wrapped in sailcloth shrouds, weighted with cannonballs, and dumped unceremoniously overboard.

Creighton's eyes sought out the body of Captain Pierce. He still lay where he had fallen. Someone had been considerate enough to lay him out straight, set pennies on his eyelids, and place his one arm across his chest.

Beyond the captain's corpse, through the hole that had been blasted in the *Amity*'s gunwales, Creighton caught sight of the stern of the privateers' vessel, and of the name that was painted there: *Revenge.* So Captain Pierce had had his chance to strike back at the rogues who had defeated and disarmed him before, and he had failed—not because he lacked skill or courage, but because the Americans had resorted to treachery and deceit.

A sailor was preparing to wrap Captain Pierce's body in canvas, but Arnold stayed him. "Let him be until we've the time to give him a proper funeral." He kicked a broken spar out of the way and stepped to the rail of the quarterdeck. "Your attention, gentlemen!" Creighton secretly scoffed at his use of the term to address a pack of pirates. The Americans paused in their various tasks to listen. "I offer these conditions to the crew of the captured vessel. Those who renounce their loyalty to the king and embrace the Patriot cause will be released."

The *Amity*'s men stared sullenly at him. Creighton was confident that few, if any, of them would take the offer. Englishmen were not so quick as Americans to forswear their allegiance to their king.

"Of those who agree to these terms," Arnold went on, "half will be transferred to the *Revenge*. The other half will stay aboard the *Amity*, along with some of my crew, to sail her to the port of New Orleans."

"New Orleans?" Creighton turned to Peter, who stood— or rather loomed—next to him. "New Orleans is in Spanish territory!"

The giant shrugged. "We Patriots had to go somewhere. The Spanish have no more love for England than we do."

"When you saw the rebellion was doomed, why did you not just surrender?"

Peter laughed. "You may as well ask why we didn't just hang ourselves, and save King George the trouble."

"The English don't hang prisoners of war," Creighton replied indignantly. "Only traitors."

"According to the king and his ministers, that's what we are." He nodded toward the main deck. "And that's what they'll be." Creighton followed his gaze. Every man of the *Amity*'s crew who could walk had asked to be unchained; they were crowding about the quarterdeck steps, swearing on the Bible to be loyal to the American cause—every man but one. Lieutenant Hale stood rigidly at the base of the mainmast, the expression on his face as hard and unyielding as the iron shackles that were clamped to his ankles.

Hale was locked in the captain's cabin, along with Colonel Gower. Creighton waited for someone to tell him what to do. When no one did, he retired to his cabin and lay down on his bunk. Though ordinarily he despised having to follow orders, he would actually have welcomed an order or two just now, for he was feeling all adrift, like a ship cut loose from its anchor and tossed about, not by wind, but by the whims of Fate. Each time he was sure that his situation was as bad as it could be, he was plunged into some new and even more dire circumstance.

First he had been banished to Carolina, which would have been cruel enough, but then he had found himself condemned to the still more distant and dismal outpost of

Florida. And now he was to be dragged even farther from civilization, to a place that was not even British territory, a place where he would be surrounded not only by red Indians and alligators but by Spaniards and Yankeys.

The *Amity* had been so badly crippled by cannon fire that Creighton assumed it would be several days before she could be made seaworthy. He prayed that while they were dead in the water, another British vessel would turn up—preferably one that was better armed—and make the Americans pay in blood for their villainy.

But somehow the privateers, aided by their new conscripts, managed to get the schooner under way in only a few hours. Soon after they set sail, the giant entered Creighton's cabin—this time in the normal fashion, for the door could no longer be bolted. He nodded amiably. "I hope you don't object to a roommate."

Creighton sat up, scowling. "As a matter of fact I do. I don't like sharing accommodations with anyone, let alone a pirate."

Peter stared at him reproachfully. "I'm not a pirate. I'm a corporal in the Patriot army."

"Of course you are. And I'm a rear admiral in the Ethiopian navy."

"Do they have a navy?" Peter asked. Then he flushed a little and laughed. "I see. You're making a joke. Stupid me, I'm ready to believe anything." He sat on the other bunk and pulled off his boots, wincing as he did so. "These boots. They make my toes curl up like caterpillars. It's hard to find boots big enough for these feet of mine." He lifted one of the appendages in question, which, with the addition of claws and fur, would not have looked out of place on a bear.

Creighton was about to repeat his protest, but something stopped him. Perhaps it was that feeling of being alone and adrift. He felt the need of company, and unless he wished to be locked up with his uncle and Lieutenant Hale, he would have to settle, like Robinson Crusoe, for whatever company he could get.

"I warrant you're feeling about the same way my feet feel, an't you?" said Peter.

Creighton gave him an incredulous look. "What do you mean?"

"You know—free. Unbound."

Creighton had all but forgotten that he was supposed to be an indentured servant. No wonder the giant had been baffled by his high-and-mighty behavior. No servant would dare to be so cheeky. He sighed. He had always considered himself a capable actor. The theatricals that were presented semiannually were the one aspect of school in which he excelled. But he'd always been given the role of a gentleman, usually something of a dandy, such as Sir Anthony in *The Rivals*. Pretending to be lower-class and servile promised to be far more challenging and not nearly as enjoyable.

"I know all about it," Peter was saying. "That's how my father came to the Colonies—as bound servant to a surveyor. Lucky for him the man died, and he took over the trade."

Creighton yawned broadly. "Fascinating."

Peter gave him a baffled look. "Excuse me for saying so, but for a fellow who's been rescued from bondage, you don't seem to me to be very grateful."

"Grateful? You expect me to be grateful, when I'm being hauled off to no-man's-land? Couldn't you just set me ashore at Mobile or Biloxi?"

Peter stared at him again, as though uncertain whether or not he was joking. "That's English territory."

"Of course. That's the point. I *am* English, you know. What in the world will I do in New Orleans—presuming that I don't die right away from some tropical disease?"

Peter shrugged his broad shoulders. "Take up a trade?" he suggested.

"A trade? What sort of trade? Highway robbery?" Then he reminded himself that he was not playing the part of a gentleman. He sighed again, more deeply. He had been a servant for only a few hours and already he was deathly sick of it.

In the morning Creighton asked, as humbly as he could manage, whether he might talk with Colonel Gower for a few moments. Peter looked surprised. "Faith, I'd have thought you'd want no more to do with him."

"Why would you think that?"

"Well, he's the one you were indentured to, an't he?"

"Oh," Creighton said. "Yes. He is. But you see . . . he owes me a month's wages."

Peter frowned in puzzlement. "I never heard of a bound servant being paid wages."

"That's because you're an American. We do things differently in England. Now, I'm going to go see him, all right?"

Since Peter could find no reason to refuse, he let Creighton into the captain's cabin and stood guard at the door. Hale was sitting in a chair by the window, still shackled. He raised a hand in greeting, but before he could say anything, the colonel sprang up from the captain's desk and confronted Creighton. "Have you learned anything?"

"Learned anything? How do you mean?"

"Any information that may be of use to us?"

"I didn't know I was expected to be a spy."

"You're an Englishman. You're among the enemy. You are expected to learn whatever you can about them."

Creighton thought a moment. "I know that we're headed for New Orleans."

The colonel sniffed. "I could have guessed that. Anything else?"

Creighton shook his head. "Listen, I can't go on pretending to be a servant, as you told me to. It's too . . ."

His uncle glared at him. "Too what?"

"Too embarrassing. Too demeaning."

"More demeaning than being locked up?" the colonel demanded. He gestured toward Hale. "More demeaning than being shackled, like a common criminal? If they believe you're nothing more than a bound boy, they'll not regard you as a threat. They'll talk freely in front of you."

"But I don't want—" Creighton protested.

Gower put up a hand to silence him. "Soft! They'll hear you." He hooked a finger in Creighton's waistcoat and drew the boy nearer to him, so near that Creighton could make out for the first time the color of his uncle's narrow, deep-set eyes. They were a cold gray, like lead. "Now you listen to me. It doesn't matter what you want or do not want. We will need an ally outside these walls. God knows if I had a choice, I would not have chosen you. But you're all we have. And the more you ingratiate yourself with our enemies, the more they come to trust you, the more valuable you will be to us."

Creighton stared at the colonel incredulously, as though the man had suggested he ingratiate himself with the alligators. "You want me to make *friends* with the Americans?"

"Not in reality, of course. You will only seem so. You will, as it were, be flying false colors."

Like those of highwaymen, the daring exploits of spies had always held a good deal of romantic appeal for Creighton. But the prospect of turning spy himself gave him pause. It wasn't that he was a coward; he might have undertaken the task if it had been for a good cause. Doing it because his uncle ordered him to did not seem a particularly good cause. But perhaps the chance to strike back at the people who killed his father was. "I don't know. I'm not certain I can do it."

"Neither am I. But I suggest you try."

"And if I don't?" The colonel was hardly in a position to demand anything of him, after all, or to punish him if he didn't comply.

He expected the colonel to respond with anger, with an order, a command. Instead the man said calmly, "Clearly it's no use appealing to your sense of honor or duty, so let me just point out that sooner or later—whether it is through ransom or exchange or some other means—we will gain our freedom and return to English soil."

"So?"

"So," the colonel went on, with the confident air of a cardplayer who knows he holds the winning hand, "I imagine you'll want to go with us."

Creighton did his best to bluff. "And what will my mother say when she learns that you've deserted me?"

The colonel shrugged. "How would she learn it? England is a long way off. I can write to her whatever I like, and she has no alternative but to believe it—just as she believed what I told her about your father."

"My father? What do you mean?"

The colonel turned away and seated himself again at the captain's desk. Creighton started after him. "What do you mean?" he demanded.

Lieutenant Hale stepped forward and blocked his way. "Gently, lad. Calm yourself."

"I want to know what he means!" Creighton leaned over the desk. "Did you lie to us in some way about my father's fate?" he shouted. "Did you?"

The door to the cabin opened and the giant strode in, his pistol drawn and cocked. "What's going on here?" He trained the gun on Hale, who was restraining Creighton.

The lieutenant let go of the boy and shuffled back a few steps. "He's a bit upset, that's all."

Peter glanced at Creighton. "What's the trouble? Won't he part with your wages?"

Creighton was so agitated that he might have blurted out the truth had his uncle not spoken first. "Wages? Is that what you came here for? Why did you not simply say so?" The colonel dug a handful of coins from the pocket of his waistcoat and tossed them onto the desktop. "There. You see how simple everything is if you just make it clear what you want?"

Creighton stared at the coins. They were, of course, not what he wanted at all. What he wanted was to go home—that, and to know whatever it was that his uncle was withholding from him about his father. But it was clear that the only way he could hope to obtain either of those things was to give the colonel what *he* wanted.

"An't that right?" Peter asked.

Creighton looked up at him, confused. "What?"

Peter pointed to the coins. "An't that what you had coming?"

"Oh. Yes." Hesitantly, Creighton picked up a shilling and turned it between his fingers. Though the money was only a pretense, he had the uneasy feeling that if he accepted it, if he kept up the pretense, he would be agreeing to act as the colonel's spy. Yet what choice did he have? As he thrust the money into his waistcoat pocket, he caught the look on his uncle's face—the complacent look of a man who had, as usual, gotten his way—and for the first time Creighton had an inkling of what it felt like to be a servant.

Chapter SIX

*I*n the days that followed, several other vessels were sighted, but always they were far off and posed no threat. On the fourth day after the *Amity*'s capture, she and the *Revenge* sailed through a narrow strait and into a body of water several miles across.

Though Creighton's command of any geography beyond the British Isles was vague, he did recall that New Orleans lay at the mouth of the Mississippi River. If this was the Mississippi, then perhaps the stories of how much bigger things were in America were true. But Peter revealed that they had, in fact, sailed into a lake he called Pontchartrain. "If you go up the Mississippi, you have to fight the current, plus a headwind. It can take a month, sometimes, to reach New Orleans that way. This way is easier."

The ships crossed the lake and anchored a hundred yards or so from the south shore. In the morning, a party of men rowed off, then returned late in the day with four flat-bottomed scows. The crew loaded them with the *Amity*'s cargo—mostly bales of cotton and tobacco and barrels of indigo and rice that the ship had taken on in Charles Town, plus farming implements and household goods originally meant for the settlers in the Florida colony.

Benedict Arnold came aboard the *Amity* to supervise the work. When a sailor carrying a sack of salt tripped and dropped his load, it landed on a cannon block and split open, sending salt cascading across the deck. Just as abruptly, Arnold's temper burst forth, and he showered the sailor with a torrent of abuse and invective. He came within an inch of striking the man, but contented himself with seizing the poor fellow by the nape of the neck and sending him staggering back toward the hold.

"Does he always have such a short fuse?" Creighton asked the giant.

Peter winced a little, as though this were a sore subject. "He tries to keep it in check, but the longer he does, the worse it is when it finally breaks loose. It's been a source of grief for him more than once. But it's also what makes him such a fearless and fearsome fighter."

"Not fearsome enough, it seems. After all, it was his side who lost the war."

Peter's temper was clearly less quick than his commander's. He merely shrugged and grinned. "It an't lost yet."

Within a few hours the barges were piled so high with goods that the water threatened to slop over their gunwales. By the time half a dozen crew members had climbed into each one, the boats had no more than four inches of freeboard.

"I hope you don't expect me to ride in one of those," Creighton said.

"Poh, there's nothing to fret about," Peter said blithely. "Come on."

They climbed down the cargo net and into one of the barges. When Peter stepped aboard, its hull seemed to sink another inch or two. As they rowed away from the ship, Creighton looked back to see his uncle and Lieutenant Hale, escorted by two guards, climbing into another boat.

The crew piloted the barge toward a crescent-shaped fort made of wooden posts sunk into the ground, with planks nailed to them. But before they reached it, they swung about and headed into the mouth of a narrow waterway that disappeared between stands of unfamiliar trees, many of them draped with long strands of some gray substance. "Spanish moss," Peter informed him, even though he hadn't asked. "And them are cypress trees."

The waterway could not accurately be called a river, for the brown water in it seemed not to be flowing at all. It was more like a winding canal. The banks were twenty feet apart at most, and half that expanse of water was choked with reeds—and, Creighton guessed, with snakes and alligators as well. He kept as far from the gunwales as the piles of cargo would allow.

"This here is Bayou San Juan," Peter said. "It takes us inland four or five miles." Though Creighton had no notion what a bayou was, he could not have been persuaded to admit it. Peter told him anyway. "*Bayou* is an Indian word,

I believe. 'Tis like a river, only instead of the water flowing out of it and into the lake, it's the other way around."

The passage soon grew so narrow that the crew were forced to ship their oars and take up poles. Something pricked the back of Creighton's neck and he slapped at the spot instinctively. "Mosquitoes," Peter told him. "They get thick as mustard when dusk comes on."

"I *know* what mosquitoes are," Creighton replied irritably. "We have them in England, you know."

"But," said Peter, with a trace of pride, "the ones here are bigger, I warrant."

"No doubt," Creighton muttered. "And so are the fools."

It was gloomy amid the overhanging trees, and became more so as the sun sank lower. At the same time the bayou grew ever narrower and more shallow. Creighton began to suspect that they had taken a wrong turn somewhere. Surely nothing could lie at the end of such a dismal corridor except perhaps their doom. Yet the sailors went on poling the scow through the dark water, seemingly unconcerned.

Just when it seemed that both the daylight and the water would give out entirely, a clearing appeared on their left. In it stood a long, low structure built of boards. Creighton looked about for other buildings and saw none. "*This* is New Orleans?" he asked incredulously. It was even more primitive than he'd imagined.

Peter seemed amused. "No, this here's a warehouse. We've got to hike another two miles overland to get to town."

Creighton glared at him. "You've no call to make me feel stupid!"

Peter seemed taken aback by the accusation. "I'm sorry. I never meant to."

"I'd like to see how well *you'd* fare in a place like London!"

"I'm sorry," the giant repeated. " 'Pon my honor, I wasn't making fun. I was only trying to be helpful."

"Well," said Creighton, a little less harshly, "stop trying, all right?"

The barges that had preceded them were tied up along the bank, and their crews were transferring the cargo to the warehouse. Creighton's boat drifted up behind the others and was made fast to a cypress trunk. Seemingly without effort, Peter scooped up a hundred-pound sack of coffee beans under each arm and stepped ashore. Creighton followed, empty-handed.

By the time the barges were unloaded, dusk was upon them—and so were the mosquitoes. The sailors began passing around a clay pot; each man dipped out a handful of some thick substance and smeared it on his hands and face. Peter scooped his share from the container and handed it to Creighton, who took one whiff of it and nearly dropped the pot. "What *is* that?"

"You really want me to tell you?" Peter asked as he nonchalantly slathered the smelly stuff over every inch of exposed skin. "I wouldn't want you feeling stupid again."

Creighton was glad that it was growing dark; it hid

the smile that he couldn't restrain. "Yes, I really want to know."

" 'Tis bacon grease."

Creighton winced. "It's also rancid." He thrust the pot back into Peter's hands. "I'm not about to anoint myself with that."

The giant stared at him, then at the pot, and then shrugged. "As the dying tailor said, suit yourself."

The party started off through the trees, following a broad, well-worn path. Before they had traveled a hundred yards, Creighton began to regret his decision to forgo the bacon grease. The mosquitoes were so numerous and so merciless that he felt almost the way he had felt aboard the *Amity*, after the cannonballs struck and the air was filled with deadly debris. He wanted to cry out, to fall to his knees and cover his head with his arms.

He drew from his sleeve that accessory carried by every true gentleman, the handkerchief. He draped it over his neck and drew the ends together under his chin, like a wimple. The thin linen offered little protection; the mosquitoes pierced it like so many pins. The one thing the cloth did impede was his breathing. The hot, humid air had made him short of breath to begin with; now he felt as though he were suffocating. He pulled the cloth aside and drew a deep breath, only to inhale a horde of mosquitoes that set him coughing and choking.

"Are you all right?" Peter asked.

Creighton couldn't manage a reply—which was just as well, considering his ugly mood. He knew that the sensible thing would be to give in and armor himself with rancid grease, but his pride wouldn't let him. He wondered whether his uncle, who was somewhere in the rear of the party, under close guard, had deigned to daub himself with the stuff. He doubted it.

A crashing, crackling sound off to his right, accompanied by savage grunts, drove the mosquito problem from his mind. "What's that?" he demanded in an urgent whisper, imagining Indians.

"Wild pigs, like enough," Peter replied.

Another building appeared ahead, silhouetted against the sky. "The brickyard," Peter said, no doubt to save Creighton the embarrassment of mistaking it for New Orleans.

Creighton had not pictured New Orleans as the sort of place to have bricks. He had imagined it, in his more optimistic moments, as a cluster of squalid log huts. After another interminable half hour of stumbling over tree roots and swatting mosquitoes, he got his first inkling of how far off the mark he was.

The trees dwindled and they emerged onto a broad flood plain. A hundred yards ahead lay a palisade of upright logs, surrounded by a ditch. Within the palisade some five hundred houses were lined up, like so many well-trained soldiers, in half a dozen neat rows, parallel to the river. A low bank of earth a thousand yards or more in length lay between the buildings and the broad expanse of the Mississippi.

The streets of the city were not lighted by lamps as the streets of Bristol were, but the candlelight that shone from the windows of the houses seemed familiar and inviting. They approached a gate in the log wall. General Arnold identified himself, and the guards allowed them to pass through. "Why do they need a palisade?" Creighton asked.

"To keep out the Indians and the English."

The way Peter lumped the two together, as though they were equally barbarous and detestable, irked Creighton. "What do they have to fear from England? The two countries aren't at war."

"Not yet. But General Arnold says it's only a matter of time. He says the Brits would love to take New Orleans, because then they'd control the mouth of the Mississippi. They'd also have us Patriots right where they want us: in prison, or at the end of a rope."

The houses of New Orleans were not quite as grand, overall, as those in Charles Town, but neither were they especially small or shabby. The more modest dwellings were covered in clapboard, with wooden shakes on the roofs. The better ones were built of timbers with bricks laid up between them, and were roofed with slate or tile. The walls of some had been plastered with stucco and whitewashed.

They all had three things in common. One was a drainage ditch—usually overgrown with reeds—that circled the property. The second was a wide veranda, similar to those he'd seen in Charles Town. The third was the foundation: rather than being set on a solid footing of stone or brick, the houses were raised up on pilings, sometimes as much as six or eight feet above the level of the dirt street.

Obviously the wall of earth that bordered the river sometimes failed to keep the Mississippi from straying beyond its banks and into the territory it had once occupied.

By the time the company reached the open square at the heart of the city, the men had begun to disperse and go their separate ways, until all that remained besides Creighton were the giant and the general, along with the two prisoners and their guards.

Arnold eyed the colonel and the lieutenant thoughtfully. "We'll try confining these two in the Cabildo House. If they cause any trouble, we can transfer them to the prison."

Colonel Gower stepped forward, contemptuously pushing aside the guard who tried to restrain him. "I protest, sir, in the strongest terms! It is contrary to the rules of war to confine an officer who has given his word not to escape!"

"Perhaps," said Arnold. "But you said yourself that we are not at war. You can't have it both ways. Besides, you continue to keep our officers, including General Washington, locked away in prison cells. When you allow them their liberty, we will do the same for you, not before." He turned to Peter. "Do you suppose Mr. Franklin can find room for another stray?"

"Like enough." The giant beckoned to Creighton, who was still busy batting at the air around him. "Come on."

Creighton hesitated, gazing after his uncle and Lieutenant Hale, who were being ushered toward a brick-and-timber building on one side of the square. If he went with Peter, he had no idea what he might be letting himself in for. On the other hand, he knew exactly what awaited him if he cast his lot with the colonel, and it was not a happy prospect.

He set off after Peter, whose seven-league strides had already carried him a stone's throw away. Though Creighton had some difficulty catching up, at least the quick pace left some of the mosquitoes behind. "Where are we going?" he asked breathlessly.

"To Dr. Franklin's home, on Royal Street."

"Franklin? Is he any relation of Benjamin Franklin?"

"He's one and the same."

Creighton was so surprised that he halted in his tracks—until the halo of mosquitoes encircled his head again; then he broke into a trot to evade them. "I thought he was dead."

"Dr. Franklin? He's the least dead of anyone I know. I believe all the electrical energy he's soaked up keeps him going. So, they've heard of him in England, have they?"

"Of course. In fact, I venture to say that he's better known there than any other American. I wasn't aware he was a doctor, though."

"I believe it's what they call an honorary title. Folk say he's a genius. Personally, I wouldn't recognize genius if it sprang up and bit me, but I do know he's a devilish clever fellow."

"Is that so? Back home, those I associated with regarded him as something of a rustic buffoon."

Peter was silent for a time, as though digesting the remark. Finally he said, "Then I'd say you associated with the wrong sort of folk."

Nothing Creighton had seen in America so far had been anything like he expected, and Dr. Franklin's house was no exception. It was unimpressive, both in its size and its construction. Though it stood on brick pillars, the walls were merely cypress boards.

"There's no light in his room," Peter said. "He's probably gone to bed." He led Creighton around to the rear of the house, where the windows were lighted.

"This is hardly the sort of place I would have expected to find a former ambassador to England and France living," Creighton observed.

"I warrant he has trouble affording even this. He's in the same boat as most of the Patriots; most everything he had—money, possessions, property—was taken by the Brits."

"Oh," said Creighton. "I didn't know."

"I didn't suppose you would." They climbed the stairs to the veranda. Three doors opened onto the porch; Peter knocked at the center one. It was opened a moment later by a slight, dark-haired girl of about Creighton's age, who wore a linen cap and an apron over her dress.

"Peter!" she cried. "You have returned safe and sound!" She was about to throw her arms around him, but then she seemed to think better of it. She retreated a step and hung her head, her hands clasped together tightly as though restraining each other. "Will you come in?" she said, more demurely. Her heavy accent told Creighton that she was neither English nor American; nor was it like any Spanish accent he'd heard. He put her down as French, and she shortly proved him right.

Peter had made no move to enter. He stood rooted to the porch, his hat in his huge hands. "I didn't want to— I only—"

The girl abruptly became animated again, waving a hand at them impatiently. *"Vite, vite,* before *les moustiques* invite themselves in as well!"

Peter ducked through the doorway and Creighton followed. Waving a towel at the mosquitoes in their wake, the girl slammed the door shut behind them. The interior of the house was arranged very differently from the typical English dwelling. There were no hallways. They had entered a sort of foyer, and from it doors led directly into the other rooms of the house.

The girl led them through the dining room and into the pantry. "I was just putting some things away," she said. Though the pantry was small, an open window kept it from being intolerably stuffy. Creighton wondered at first why the room was not swarming with mosquitoes. Then he saw that the window was covered with loosely woven fabric that allowed air to pass through, but not insects.

"One of Dr. Franklin's inventions," Peter said. "Here's another." He gestured at a curious contraption that hung from the ceiling. It consisted of a boxlike frame of wood, covered with strips of the same sort of fabric that was on the window. Atop the box was a dish full of water. The ends of the fabric strips were draped over the edge of the dish.

"What is it?" Creighton asked.

"He calls it an evap-o-ra-tive cooler," Peter said, pronouncing the words carefully. "You see, the water runs down over the cloth and . . . and . . ." He trailed off. "And somehow that keeps the food in the box cool. I don't really understand it. You'll have to ask Dr. Franklin. As I said, he's a devilish clever fellow."

"And you, Peter, are a devilish rude fellow," the girl chided him. "You have been gone for two weeks, and all you can talk about is Dr. Franklin's inventions? Who have you brought with you?"

"I'm sorry," the giant mumbled, shamefaced. "You know when it comes to social things, I'm like a dog in a dancing school."

"Then I shall have to make up for it." She curtsied awkwardly to Creighton, as though she had only just learned how. "*Je suis* Sophie Doucet."

Creighton was more accustomed to ignoring housemaids or ordering them about than to being introduced to them. He stared at her a moment before he remembered that he was supposed to be a servant, too. He turned to her and bowed slightly. "Creighton Brown."

To his surprise, her brown eyes went wide and one work-reddened hand flew to her mouth, as though he'd said something scandalous. *"Bonté!"* she breathed. *"Votre visage!"* She passed her hand across her features. "Your face!"

Puzzled, Creighton put his fingers to his cheek. The skin was a mass of bumps, as though he'd suffered a sudden and extreme outbreak of pimples. His face was hot to the touch, too, partly from the bites and partly from embarrassment. He was about to respond with some unpleasant remark, as he normally did in such situations, but the girl held up her hand.

"I have something that will help." She turned to a set of shelves and, standing on tiptoe, took down a glass jar filled with a salve of some sort. "Rub *un petit peu*—a small amount—on your face. It will make the swelling go down, and make the itching less."

Creighton regarded the salve dubiously. "It's not bacon grease, is it?"

She laughed. "*Non, non.* It is comfrey and myrtle. You will smell very pleasant." She looked up at Peter's well-greased countenance and wrinkled her nose. "Unlike some others I could name." At once she bit her lip and hung her head again. "Ah, *pardonnez-moi*," she said meekly. "That was a thoughtless thing for me to say."

But Peter did not appear offended so much as baffled. "What's come over you?"

She blinked innocently at him. "Whatever do you mean?"

"Well, I mean . . . I don't remember you ever begging pardon for anything before, least of all for your . . ."

She gave a slight, mischievous smile. "For my sharp tongue?"

"Well . . . yes."

The girl said soberly, "Ah, but I am not the same Sophie Doucet to whom you bade farewell a few weeks ago."

"You—you an't?"

"*Mais non.* I have embarked upon a regimen of self-improvement."

Understanding dawned suddenly on the giant's face. "You've been talking to Dr. Franklin."

"*Oui.* He has devised a plan by which I may improve my character."

"A plan?"

Sophie nodded enthusiastically. "Each week I am to devote myself to cultivating one of thirteen basic virtues: frugality, sincerity, tranquillity, et cetera. This week it is *humilité.*"

"Humility."

"*Oui.*" She bit her lip again, thoughtfully this time. "I am beginning to think that I may have to allow two weeks for this one."

Peter frowned. "I know that I an't a fraction as intelligent as Dr. Franklin, but I liked your character the way it was."

Sophie made another awkward curtsy. "*Merci.* But I have become aware that my behavior is sometimes not so very . . . *comment dit-on?* . . . so very ladylike." She turned back to Creighton and inquired in a ladylike fashion, "The ointment makes it better, *n'est-ce pas?*"

"Yes," Creighton admitted grudgingly.

"*Bon.* You will be staying with us?"

Creighton glanced rather sullenly at Peter. "It seems I have nothing to say in the matter."

"Could you make shift to put him up for tonight?" Peter asked. "In the morning Dr. Franklin can decide whether he's to stay."

Sophie nodded. "Where are you from?" she asked Creighton, and then, apparently considering this too blunt and unladylike, quickly added, "If you do not mind my asking."

"Bristol."

Sophie tilted her head to one side. "Bristol?" she repeated, though she pronounced it *Breestol*. "Where is that—if you do not mind my asking?"

"On the western coast."

"The western coast of what?"

Creighton stared at her incredulously. "Why, England, of course."

Her expression changed from one of amiable curiosity to something much harsher and more hostile. "England? *Vous êtes anglais?*" She turned to Peter with a disapproving, almost accusing look. "You did not tell me he was English!"

━━━◆✕◆━━━

Chapter SEVEN

*P*eter shifted uncomfortably; his big hands nearly crushed the brim of his hat. "It an't as though he's a soldier, Sophie. He an't even here of his own free will. He was indentured. I thought you'd . . . . well . . . sympathize."

"Did you?" She surveyed Creighton with such distaste that he felt a bit ashamed, though he wasn't certain of what. Finally Sophie shrugged. "My plan does not call for me to practice tolerance until next week, but I suppose I could begin a little early. I will make the guest room ready."

When she was gone, Creighton said, "What reason does she have to resent the English? She's no Yankey."

"Her mother and her father were Acadians," Peter said. Creighton, who hated to admit ignorance on any subject, didn't ask what Acadians were. Peter told him anyway. "They belonged to a French settlement in Nova Scotia—which is someplace in Canada, I believe."

"I know that," Creighton put in peevishly.

"Well, anyway, the Brits kicked them out. Her folks were split up. The father went to France, or somewhere. The mother was put on a ship for New Orleans, but she never made it. Died of a fever or something—but not before she'd give birth to Sophie. Some other family took her in, but they died, too, from the yellow fever. Since then she's been passed around from one household to another, and all of 'em treated her more like a servant than a daughter. But you'd know what that's like, I warrant."

Though Creighton still resented being considered a servant, there was some truth in what Peter said, for in these past weeks he'd been passed from one set of uncaring hands to another, like a coin of little worth.

"She does say, though," Peter went on, "that Dr. Franklin has used her very kindly, even though she's only hired help."

Creighton knew what it was like to be treated kindly, too, though with each month that went by since his father's death, it became harder for him to recall. Major Brown had had the rare ability to influence and inspire the men who served under him, not by threatening or haranguing them, but by treating them fairly, and with respect. He had used the same tactics on his son.

Creighton's mother was fond of telling anyone who would listen that she had always been good to her son, but what she called kindness was really indulgence. She had given him everything he wanted and withheld the one thing he really needed—her affection.

The room Sophie had prepared for him was small and modestly furnished, but pleasant enough. There were no mosquito barriers on the windows, but the bed was enclosed in a low frame made of cane, over which loosely woven fabric was draped.

"If you are hungry, there is bread and cheese in the *garde-manger*," the girl said brusquely, and departed. Creighton was hungry, but it was a distant, feeble complaint compared with the weariness that engulfed him, weighing him down like an iron cloak. He dragged his boots off his feet and then, too exhausted to undress further, he blew out the candle, pawed his way through the mosquito netting, stretched gratefully out on the feather bed, and fell instantly asleep.

When he woke, the plastered walls of the room were yellow with sunlight. Creighton lay still a few moments, getting his bearings. Then he pulled aside the linen hangings, shoved a foot into one of his boots, and abruptly yanked it out again as the sole of his foot encountered something prickly—something that moved.

Startled, he upended the boot and shook it vigorously. Out tumbled a nasty-looking creature unlike anything he'd ever seen before. It bore a certain resemblance to a crayfish, but with a thinner, lighter-colored body and a long, segmented tail that curled over upon itself. The thing scuttled away across the floor. Creighton shuddered and pounded both boots vigorously on the floor before slipping them on.

Sophie had filled the porcelain pitcher on the washstand. Creighton poured water into the basin and washed his hands and face. Though his skin was still bumpy, the swelling and the itching had mostly disappeared. Now, if only he had a hot bath, a clean set of clothing, and a decent meal, he might feel almost human.

To his surprise the house appeared deserted. In the pantry he discovered the bread and cheese Sophie had mentioned, inside the evaporative cooler, but he found nothing to wash it down with except a pitcher of water. Surely there must be ale somewhere, or cider, at least.

He returned to the foyer and called, "Sophie!" There was no reply. Exasperated at being left to fend for himself, he called more loudly, "Hello! Is anyone here?"

From behind a closed door came a voice that was assuredly not Sophie's. "What's all the commotion?"

Creighton yanked open the door, revealing a large chamber that appeared to be a combination bedroom and sitting room. In the center of it was an elegant writing desk.

Seated at the desk was a rotund elderly man, entirely naked except for a nightcap that sat at a rakish angle above a broad forehead. Perched on his prominent nose was a curious pair of gold-rimmed spectacles with square lenses, each lens made of two separate pieces of glass.

The man looked up from the sheet of paper on which he had been writing and peered at Creighton through the upper half of the spectacles. "Who are you?"

Creighton's tavern companions back home had been an uninhibited, even profane lot, so he was not easily shocked or flustered, but the sight of someone sitting in the altogether, not in a Turkish bath or in a mineral spa but at a writing desk, threw him off balance.

"Well?" said the man, who seemed not at all self-conscious about his lack of attire.

"Um . . . I'm Creighton Brown. I'm sorry to have disturbed you."

He would have made a quick retreat, but the man said calmly, "I'm Dr. Franklin. Come in. Close the door. I thought I had locked it, but at my age one can never be certain of anything, not even of getting up in the morning." He gestured at an upholstered chair; unlike the furnishings in Colonel Gower's chambers back in Charles Town, these had been designed with comfort in mind. "You're the bound boy from the captured vessel."

The remark put Creighton even more off balance. "How did you know that?"

Franklin smiled slyly. "I'm a newspaperman. I make it

my business to know what goes on. I understand you need a place to stay."

Creighton nodded. "Just until I can find a way home."

"Home?"

Creighton had meant England, but he realized that this wasn't in keeping with his role. He had supposedly sold himself into servitude in order to come to the New World. "Carolina," he said, though the notion of returning there was only a little less abhorrent than the prospect of remaining in Louisiana.

"Why would you want to return to English territory? Here, you're free."

Creighton nearly laughed. Free? He had been free in England. Now he was imprisoned in a foreign land. "Free to do what?"

"Whatever you like. What skills do you have?"

Creighton was at a loss for an answer. He had been brought up to be a gentleman, and gentlemen were not expected to have any particular skills, aside from riding and shooting.

"Can you read?" Franklin prompted him.

"Of course."

Franklin shoved toward him the sheet of paper on which he had been writing. "Read that."

Creighton snatched up the page and impatiently scanned the slightly shaky but precise handwriting. "I have concluded," he read, "that there never was a good war or a bad peace. It seems to me that wars are always waged not for the sake of some ideal but for the sake of gain."

"A passage from my memoirs," Franklin said. "Though I can't imagine who, aside from the two of us, will ever read them."

Creighton tossed the paper onto the table. "Was my reading satisfactory?"

"Flawless."

"I can also read Latin and Greek, if you want to know."

Franklin raised an eyebrow. "Well, well. What an oddity. A servant who not only reads the classics but also has a superior, arrogant manner."

"I wasn't brought up to be a servant."

"Oh? Then you indentured yourself only in order to come to America? What attracted you here so strongly?"

"I was not attracted here so much as I was repelled from there."

Franklin smiled appreciatively. "Ah. You understand the principles of magnetism, too. You must have had a good education." He sat back and drummed the tips of his thick fingers together thoughtfully. "I may be able to use you."

"Use me? To do *work*, you mean?"

"You have some objection to work? What sort of servant are you?"

"A poor one."

"So I would imagine. Well, I'm sorry to disappoint you, but if you expect to stay here, you must be willing to earn your keep. I can't afford to take in idlers."

Creighton scowled. "You'd turn me out? I was told you were a kind man."

"Were you?" Franklin laughed. "I would like to think so. But allowing you to be a leech would be no kindness."

Creighton got to his feet. "Then I'll leave."

"And go where?" Franklin asked, with what sounded like genuine curiosity. When Creighton did not reply, the old man motioned toward the chair. "Sit down." He reached for a deck of playing cards that lay on one side of the writing desk. "You look like a cardplayer to me. Am I correct?"

Creighton eyed the cards warily. "I know a bit about it."

"Good. Let me offer this proposal. We'll play a hand of commerce. If you should win, you may stay on here as long as you like, with no obligation. If I should happen to win, you will still get to stay, but you will work for me in my printing shop. Fair enough?"

Lieutenant Hale had taught Creighton some valuable things about cardplaying. One was never to let the expression on your face give you away. So he suppressed the confident grin that threatened to spread across his features and said soberly, "Fair enough."

Franklin shuffled and dealt the cards clumsily, as though his hands were gouty or arthritic. He dealt three cards faceup and three facedown. Creighton picked up the unknown cards and fanned them out, revealing a knave of hearts, a deuce of spades, and a nine of clubs. He discarded the deuce and drew a second knave from the remaining three cards. He found it even harder to repress that confident grin now.

To his surprise, Franklin discarded nothing and drew nothing. Instead he rapped on the desk to indicate that he was ready. Creighton must have let his surprise show, for Franklin shrugged his bulky, naked shoulders and said, "I'm content with the cards I have. Shall we show them?"

Smugly, Creighton spread his cards face up on the desk. "Two knaves."

Franklin nodded gravely. "Well. You're a lucky fellow." Assuming the matter was settled, Creighton started to rise, but Franklin calmly waved him back into the chair. "However," he said, with a wry, unexpected smile, "as you surely know if you have followed the course of the late rebellion, the knaves always lose, and the kings"— One by one he proceeded to lay out three of them—"always win."

This time Creighton made no attempt to mask his expression. He leaned across the table, his face flushed with anger. "That's not possible! You must have—" He stopped short of saying the word that was on his tongue; he had learned from the knights of the tavern how serious a matter it was to accuse another player of trickery.

"Cheated?" Franklin said. With an innocent expression on his broad face, he spread his bare arms wide. "I assure you, I had nothing up my sleeve."

Creighton stood abruptly, and his chair toppled to the floor with a crash. "Nevertheless," he said, his voice rough with emotion, "it was not a fair contest, and I will not abide by it."

Franklin gazed at him evenly, unperturbed. "Apparently your education was not as thorough as you've led me to believe, if they failed to teach you anything about honor."

Creighton winced, as though he'd been prodded by the point of a dagger. Even in his unreasonable state of mind, he recognized how shrewd the old man was, to aim his barb at the very spot where Creighton was most vulnerable. Unable to reply, he stormed out of the room. It was ironic that, although Franklin had been naked all the while, Creighton felt as though he were the one who had lost his shirt.

———◆✕◆———

Chapter EIGHT

A clattering sound drew Creighton to the pantry, where he found Sophie scrubbing her hands in a basin. Still smarting from the drubbing he'd received at cards, he snapped, "Where have *you* been?"

Sophie glanced up in surprise. "What gives you the right to ask?" she demanded, forgetting for the moment all about humility. She took a deep breath and, with obvious effort, offered a more demure reply. "I was in the printing shop. Was there something you wanted?"

"A drink—of something besides water."

"I am very sorry, but the doctor does not approve of"—she hesitated, searching for the proper term—"strong beverages."

Creighton stared at her. "Just what does he consider a 'strong beverage'?"

"Anything besides water, I am afraid."

Creighton shook his head in disgust. "Peter says he's considered a genius; if you ask me, he's simply daft."

Sophie frowned. "I do not know this word."

"Crackbrained." Creighton twirled a finger alongside his head. "*Fou.*"

She gave him a contemptuous look and went back to scrubbing her ink-stained hands. "If you think that, then you are the one who is daff-ed."

"Oh? What would *you* call someone who receives visitors with nothing on but a nightcap?"

A snicker escaped her. "Do you mean that Dr. Franklin was the one with nothing on? Or the visitor?"

Creighton gave a grudging laugh. "Dr. Franklin, of course. Did you know he does that?"

"Well . . ." She snickered again. "I have never actually *seen* him do it. I am not permitted in his chambers, except to serve food or refreshments, or to clean. But I do know that he considers it important to . . . *comment dit-on?* . . . to allow the body to breathe."

"Hmm. I find I've always been able to breathe well enough with all my clothing on."

Sophie responded not with a snicker but with a full-fledged peal of laughter so engaging and uninhibited, so totally lacking in *humilité,* that Creighton couldn't help being caught up in it. Then Sophie seemed to recall all at once her distaste for the English. Her laughter died away; she turned her back to him and set about preparing a pot of tea.

"Tea doesn't qualify as a 'strong beverage,' in Dr. Franklin's opinion?" Creighton asked.

"Actually, this is for me." All trace of warmth was gone from her voice, but as though determined to give tolerance another try, she asked, "Would you like a cup?"

"Yes," he said, and considered adding *thank you,* but couldn't get it out.

"I will be back in a moment." She slipped out the back door and returned bearing a steaming cast-iron teakettle. "The summer kitchen is out there," she explained, indicating the direction with a tilt of her head, "in a separate building." As she filled the teapot with hot water, she said, "I believe Dr. Franklin's objection to tea is not a matter of health, but of principle."

"Oh, yes. I forgot." Creighton sighed and shook his head. "The tea tax and the Boston Tea Party happened years ago. I can't believe the Yankeys are still harboring a grudge."

Sophie gave him a severe glance. "Some injustices are difficult to forget," she said, and something in her tone told Creighton that she was not speaking of taxes on tea.

They lapsed into a silence so awkward that Creighton was almost glad when Dr. Franklin appeared in the kitchen doorway. To Creighton's relief, the old man was fully dressed, lacking only a coat. Despite the warmth of the day, he wore a curious round hat made of fur. Though a long fringe of white hair emerged from beneath the hat, Creighton suspected that the crown of Franklin's head was bald, and that the old man was vain about it. He was tempted to ask why it wasn't important for the top of the head to breathe.

Franklin gave Sophie a fatherly kiss on the forehead, then turned to beam at Creighton, rubbing his hands together as though in anticipation. "Ready to go to work?"

Sophie looked startled. "You are not putting him to work in the printing shop?"

"I am." Franklin reached down and squeezed Creighton's upper arm with a grip that was surprisingly strong for a man with gouty hands. "We have use for both his brawn and his brain." Though Creighton resented this familiarity, he was grateful, at least, that the doctor had been tactful enough not to mention the humiliating card game.

Sophie's brown eyes blinked rapidly, as though she were warding off tears. "We have done well enough until now without any help."

"Only because I've overworked you shamefully. Besides, these old arms are getting too weak to sling forms full of types about." He patted her hand gently and whispered, "Don't worry, my dear. It will work out fine; you'll see." Franklin ushered them outside and then followed, walking with a pronounced limp and wincing a little with each step. "The infernal gout is worse today," he said. "I tried

92

administering electric shock to the area, but it gave only a temporary respite from the pain."

The printing shop lay a dozen yards behind the main house. It was a squat, ugly structure made of hewn logs. "This was once used to house slaves," Franklin said. Creighton muttered to himself that its purpose had not changed much, but the old man either did not hear the comment or chose to ignore it. Sophie heard, though, and cast Creighton an unpleasant glance.

Most of the building was now occupied by two items. One was a long, low table whose surface was covered with a sheet of iron. At one end of it was a huge stack of blank paper; along the back of the table was a row of wooden bins, each containing dozens of small squares of gray metal. When Creighton looked more closely, he saw that these were pieces of lead cast with letters of the alphabet and punctuation marks, all of them backward.

The other item was a huge frame, taller than he was, constructed of oak beams six inches square, bolted together, with a wooden platform projecting from it. It had the appearance of some bizarre engine of torture—perhaps a sort of guillotine. But where the blade would have been on a guillotine, there was a massive iron screw with a handle attached to it; at the base of the screw was a thick iron plate.

"This is the printing press," Franklin told Creighton, who had already guessed as much. The old man proceeded to explain in great detail who had invented this type of press and when, and how it functioned. Bored, Creighton glanced at Sophie behind Franklin's back. She shrugged helplessly, as though to say, *He's always this way; you may as well get used to it.*

When Franklin finally finished his lecture, he turned and tapped the iron-covered table. "And this is the composing table, where Sophie sets the types." He glanced at a wooden frame filled with row after row of lead letters, and his eyebrows rose. "You've set one page already?"

Sophie gave a self-satisfied smile. "As I told you, I can manage very well alone."

"So I see," said Franklin. "But I'm afraid there's one word you've forgotten."

Sophie frowned and leaned over the form. "Where?"

"Here." Franklin picked up a long L-shaped wooden stick and, using a pair of tongs, swiftly snatched a series of letters from the type cases and lined them up on the stick to form the word *humility*.

Sophie blushed and lowered her gaze. "I am sorry. I will try more hardly."

"I know you will, my dear." He patted her hand again. "You've been handling the types with tongs, I trust, not with your fingers?"

She nodded. "It is *un peu plus lent* . . . a little more slow . . . but I am improving."

"Good. I don't want your hands ending up as mine have." He flexed his thick fingers and added, to Creighton, "The lead produces pain and stiffness in the joints, and eventually leaves the hands numb. Women once used lead as a cosmetic, you know. Over time, they lost all feeling in their faces."

Behind his back, Sophie darted a mischievous glance at Creighton that seemed to say, *There he goes, lecturing again.* Then, obviously remembering her prejudice against him, she looked away and fiddled with the composing stick.

Franklin rubbed his hands together. "Well, enough talk. It's time to work. First of all, I'd like you to carry that form over to the press for me."

Creighton gave him an incredulous look. "I thought you wanted me for my *reading* ability. I'm not accustomed to manual labor."

"Well, you will be, soon enough." Franklin gestured meaningfully at the tray full of type. When Creighton still hesitated, the old man said, under his breath, "Remember our agreement?" Creighton grudgingly bent over and seized the tray. Franklin put a hand on his arm. "Wait!" He reached down and fastened two metal clamps that held the frame together. "Mustn't forget that, or the whole thing will fall to pieces."

The tray was far heavier than Creighton had imagined. He staggered and nearly dropped it, eliciting a gasp of dismay from Sophie. "Be careful, *s'il vous plaît!* That is a whole morning's work!"

Creighton felt his face go red with anger and embarrassment, not to mention effort. He wrestled the tray onto the

95

bed of the printing press and then sat on the edge of the table, panting. While he watched, Franklin inked the type with a roller and laid a sheet of blank paper atop it. Then he slid the type and paper into place beneath the iron plate, which he called a platen. When he pulled on the handle, it turned the screw, pressing the platen against the paper and the paper against the type. After a moment he released the handle, slid the type form from under the platen, and peeled away the paper. It was no longer blank but covered with words, sentences, paragraphs.

Creighton was unaccountably and unexpectedly fascinated by the transformation. Though he had read, or at least been assigned to read, dozens of journals and books, he had never given a moment's thought to how they were made. For the first time he considered how very curious, almost incredible, it was that something as abstract and ephemeral as words and ideas could be captured and conveyed through such a mundane, mechanical process as printing.

He was struck, too, by how symmetrical, how elegantly simple the page of print looked as Franklin spread it out on the table to dry, by the stark beauty of black on white, like flakes of soot on snow, and by the heady smell of the ink, dark and bitter and a bit intoxicating—not unlike the smell of the stout beer he and his former companions drank during long, idle evenings at the alehouse.

Creighton's longing for his old haunts, which had been pushed to the back of his mind by all the events of the past few days, came to the fore again, as painful as ever, like an old wound opening. Still determined not to let his face betray him, he turned away from Dr. Franklin, only to meet the gaze of Sophie. She gave him a look of curiousity, mingled with concern.

Creighton wanted neither from her. He rose and stepped outside, where he could at least look up at the same sky that spread over England. A familiar giant figure appeared in the rear doorway of the house. "There you are!" Peter called. "Is Dr. Franklin—" At that moment Franklin emerged from the printing shop. Peter snatched off his hat and nodded respectfully to the old man. "Good morning. Mr. Jefferson sent me to fetch you. They're having a meeting at the Café."

"Very well. Wait for me, will you?" Franklin beckoned to Creighton. "Could you come inside? I have need of your brain now."

The way Franklin put it stirred something unfamiliar inside Creighton. He felt a little baffled, a little flattered, almost. He couldn't recall the last time anyone had needed him for anything more significant than to round out a game of cards or to escort some unattractive cousin to a ball. He followed the old man back into the shop.

"Would you proofread this for me?" Franklin indicated the page of crisp, orderly type. "My eyes are not what they were."

"Proofread?"

"Check the text for typographical errors—mistakes." He handed Creighton a pencil. "Please circle any you find."

Creighton scanned the page. "Half of this is in French."

"Sophie will see to that. You need concern yourself only with the English." He gave Sophie a farewell wave. "I'm needed elsewhere, my dear. I'll be back in an hour or so."

Creighton sat on a stool, rolled up his sleeves, and, with a sigh, poised the pencil over the paper. This was too much like schoolwork to suit him. But if there was one thing he was good at, it was finding flaws, and each one he discovered gave him a curious sense of satisfaction.

He was only slightly distracted from his task by the actual content of the text. For the most part it treated matters of interest only to the local residents: the price of a barrel of drinking water was being raised to twelve *reales;* a fine of two *pesos* would be levied on anyone who failed to keep the drainage ditch around his property free of refuse; a theatrical performance of that old favorite, *The Indian Father,* would be presented on Saturday next at the Maison Coquet.

Two brief items did catch his eye enough to make him linger over them. One was a proclamation from the new governor of Louisiana, Colonel de Galvez, forbidding the fighting of duels—apparently a common practice here. The other told of a prominent landowner whose home had been raided by something called *maroons.* Creighton had heard the term used only in connection with pirates, who sometimes abandoned, or marooned, their victims on desert islands—a plight he could certainly identify with.

"By *maroons,* do they mean pirates?" Creighton asked Sophie, who had taken a seat next to him in order to scan the French half of the paper.

"Escaped slaves," she said absently. "They live in the swamps."

"Oh. What about this one?" He pointed his pencil at the word *créole.* "Cree-ol-ee?"

"Cray-ole," she corrected him. "They are the descendants of the *colons*—the original settlers, both *français et espagnols.*" She frowned at the dozen or so words he had circled. "Can those all be mistakes?" She sounded exasperated, as though they were his fault.

"I wouldn't have circled them if they weren't," he replied defensively.

She gestured dramatically at the columns of French, which were practically unmarked. "*Regardez.* Two errors, *seulement.*" She glared again at Creighton's side and shook her head. "It is your English language. It is so stupid."

"Stupid?"

"*Oui.* It is so . . . what is the opposite of logical?"

"Illogical. But—"

"So illogical. Instead of one word to mean one thing, you have two or three, or eight."

"That's not so—"

She ignored him. "*En français,* when we mean it is cold, we say *froid. Simple, n'est-ce pas?* But you . . . you may say cold, or you may say chilly, or you may say freezing, or nippy, or icy, or frosty, or fridgy—"

"Frigid. But—"

"Or as cold as charity, or as cold as Christmas, or—"

Despite her complaints, Sophie obviously had a command of the English language that was good enough to talk circles around him. In self-defense, Creighton clamped his hands over his ears and hummed "Over the Hills and Far Away" until Sophie finally ran down.

When he took his hands away and glanced in her direction, her head hung down in contrition. "I am sorry. I am not much good at *humilité*, am I?"

"No." Without quite meaning to, he added, "But neither am I."

"I have noticed that. It is a pity, *n'est-ce pas*, that we cannot put our words down somewhere and correct all the mistakes before we actually say them." She rose from her stool. "Well. If you would take the form to the composing table, I will reset the words that I made wrong." As Creighton struggled to transfer the tray of type, she said, "I was not really upset with you, you know, or with your language. I was upset with myself, for making so many errors."

"I know." Creighton had to admit that, though Sophie might be no better than he was at humility, when it came to apologizing, she had him beaten by a mile. As he sat watching with interest, she undid the clasps on the type frame and then, glancing at the printed sheet for guidance, plucked out the offending letters and replaced them with the proper ones. Her quickness and dexterity amazed him. When the task was done, she stepped back and nodded in satisfaction. "*Voilà*. Now it should be *parfait*." She turned away to wipe her hands with a cloth.

Creighton bent over the table and, taking a deep breath, grabbed hold of the tray of type—forgetting to fasten the metal clamps that held it all together. When he lifted it, the rows of type collapsed. Letters and punctuation marks rained down upon his feet and upon the floor, bouncing and scattering like hailstones.

Chapter NINE

Creighton stood stunned, openmouthed, clutching the empty wooden frame. There was a moment of dead silence. Then Sophie uttered a sound that was something between a shout and a sob. It was followed by a barrage of French words that fell on Creighton as painfully and unrelentingly as the ones made of lead. Though he understood no more than one word in ten, the message behind them was clear: He was ignorant, clumsy, and useless, and what's more, so were all his countrymen and relatives, and she wished that he had never been born or, at the very least, that he had not ruined the whole North American continent by coming here.

She could not have wished it half as much as he did. He flung the form aside and headed for the door across a field of fallen type, staggering a little as the squares of lead shifted beneath his feet.

Once outside, he broke into a trot, around the house and out into the street. He had no idea where he was going. If he could have, he would have run all the way to England, back to his old life, in which nothing was asked of him, nothing expected. The beauty of no one expecting anything of you was that you couldn't possibly fail to live up to it.

He would even have settled for somewhere that was ruled by Britain. But, though he was sure there was English territory out there somewhere, probably within a few days' walk, he couldn't say exactly where, or in what direction. And even if he knew, he could never hope to make his way there on his own. If the alligators didn't do him in, the Indians would, or the maroons, or the bottomless pits of quicksand.

After wandering about aimlessly for a time, Creighton ended up on the broad street that lay nearest to the river. Ahead of him, a set of steps led to the crest of the long, low earth wall. Creighton climbed them and stood looking out over the Mississippi. Four sailing vessels were anchored in midstream, all of them flying Spanish or French flags. For a moment he entertained the notion of stowing away aboard one of them. But he would be no better off. It wouldn't take him anywhere he wanted to go, only to some equally unfamiliar, inhospitable place.

Creighton sat on the steps and put his head in his hands, trying to decide what to do next, how to avoid having to go back and face Dr. Franklin and Sophie. The complaining of his empty stomach made it difficult to think. He was as unaccustomed to going hungry as he was to working.

He fingered the coins his uncle had given him, back aboard the *Amity*, wondering whether or not the local taverns would accept British currency. Well, there was no harm in trying—unless they despised the English so much that they threw him out on his ear.

When he descended the steps, he encountered a group of barefoot boys who were heading for the river, carrying cane fishing poles. "One moment, my lad," Creighton said to the boy in the lead. "Can you tell me where to find a tavern that serves food?"

The boy regarded him with the sort of alarmed and suspicious look one might give to a leprous beggar or an escapee from an insane asylum. *"Je ne comprends pas."* He turned to his companions. *"Quelle langue parle-t-il? Espagnol?"*

One of the other boys laughed derisively. *"Non, non, c'est américain!"*

To Creighton's surprise they all began pointing at him and jeering, as though he were some grotesque or ludicrous figure. The leader started chanting a French rhyme, obviously an insulting one, and the others took up the refrain:

> *'Méricain coquin,*
> *'Billé en nanquin,*
> *Voleur de pain,*
> *Chez Miché d'Aquin!*

Creighton's knowledge of French was sketchy, but he understood the word *coquin*, which meant "rogue," and *voleur de pain,* which meant "stealer of bread." Scowling, he raised one arm threateningly. The boys scattered, but regrouped at once, still chanting, to taunt him further by poking at him with their cane poles.

Furious, he seized one of the poles and wielded it like a sword, smacking the boys' arms and legs. Under this onslaught they retreated. Creighton shouted after them, "You stupid little twits! I'm not an American! I'm English! *Anglais!* And I hope my countrymen take over your bloody town and make all of you into slaves!"

It occurred to him then that this was probably not the wisest thing to be saying in the middle of a public street. He dropped the pole and hurried off, glancing behind occasionally to make sure he wasn't being pursued by a mob of outraged Frenchmen.

Creighton walked on along the street that fronted the river without seeing anything that looked like a tavern, or at least the way an English tavern looked. Finally he found himself at the city square. Just beyond the square, the street was lined with dozens of ramshackle wooden stalls displaying foods and wares of all kinds for sale.

He approached a stall that was piled high with long, narrow loaves of bread and mounds of crusty rolls. The vendor, a plump, smiling woman, said pleasantly, *"Désirez-vous du pain aujourd'hui?"* She held up one of the appetizing loaves. *"Une baguette, peut-être?"*

Creighton nodded and fished a shilling from his waistcoat pocket.

She regarded it dubiously. *"Une pièce anglaise, hein?"*

Creighton understood that well enough: an English coin. *"Oui."*

"Du vaisseau anglais qu' ont pris les Américains?"

From the English vessel captured by the Americans. *"Oui."*

She put the coin between her teeth and bit down on it. Satisfied that it was genuine, she dropped it into the pocket of her apron and held out two loaves.

He was not accustomed to thanking anyone in any language, and had to search his brain for a moment before he could come up with *"Merci."* He tried to take the loaves, but the woman was holding fast to the other end.

"Et vous," she said, slyly, *"vous êtes une pièce anglaise aussi, n'est-ce pas?"*

You are a bit of English, too. *"Oui,"* he admitted.

"Also from the captured ship, *n'est-ce pas?*"

"Yes."

She smiled and let go of the bread. "I hope you will find *la Nouvelle-Orléans* to your liking."

He traded one of the loaves for several smoked herring from a fisherman's stall and bought a bottle of ale from a brewer. Then he sat in the shade of a tree, facing the building that Arnold had called the Cabildo, and laid into the food ravenously.

On the side of the square away from the river stood two pillories. One of them was occupied by a pathetic-looking fellow whose pudgy neck and wrists seemed too large for the holes that held him captive. Around his neck hung a placard printed in Spanish and French. As best Creighton could translate them, the words said, MY NAME IS JEAN BILLOU- ART. I AM A THIEF. I STOLE FROM THE SISTERS OF MERCY. I AM SENTENCED TO THREE DAYS' EXPOSURE AT THE PILLORY.

Apparently he had served his sentence, at least for the day, for a soldier appeared to unlock the top arm of the pillory and release him. The man shuffled off, rubbing his chafed wrists and twisting his stiff neck from side to side.

The vendors began closing up their stalls for the night. Creighton glanced up at the sun, which hung only a handsbreadth above the horizon. In less than an hour it would be dark, and the mosquitoes would begin tormenting him again, and he would have nowhere to hide.

A door at one end of the Cabildo opened and Colonel Gower and Lieutenant Hale emerged, followed by two Spanish soldiers armed with swords and muskets. The guards herded them onto the grassy parade ground at the center of the square. Creighton guessed that the prisoners were supposed to be exercising. But the iron cuffs around their ankles, linked together by a heavy chain, obviously made it hard for them to walk. Creighton almost rose to greet them, then thought better of it. Though he had nowhere else to stay, he didn't care to be locked up with them.

The colonel seemed determined to distance himself as much as possible from the guards and from his fellow prisoner. He headed across the parade ground toward the river until one of the guards called out an order in Spanish that made him turn back. As he did, he caught sight of Creighton, and paused. "Why are you here?" he demanded, his voice low and harsh.

"I've had my fill of Americans," Creighton told him.

The guard shouted to his prisoner again, and this time raised his musket to add authority. "Once we're inside," his uncle said, "come around to the rear of the building."

"Why—"

"Do it!" The colonel turned and walked off, managing somehow to maintain his military bearing despite the cumbersome chains.

By the time Creighton made his appearance at the back of the Cabildo, the daylight was fading and the mosquitoes were gathering for the kill. He couldn't determine exactly where behind that brick wall his uncle was being held. He could see nothing through the windows; they were set too high in the wall. The building had obviously been designed with defense in mind, for the windows were barred with wrought iron and equipped with massive wooden shutters.

Beneath the windows was a row of rifle ports. On the outside they were quite wide—a foot or so across. On the inside they were only three or four inches square and were closed off by a small wooden door. As Creighton stood wondering where to go, the cover on one of the rifle ports swung open, and his uncle's voice said softly, "Here! Over here!"

Creighton approached and peered into the port. He could see nothing but his uncle's mouth. "What do you want?"

"I want to know what you've found out about the rebels."

"I've hardly had time to—"

"Did they take you to Franklin's?" the colonel interrupted.

"Yes."

"Is anyone else staying there?"

"Only a French girl—a servant."

"No other rebels? Have you heard any other names mentioned?"

"No. Well, yes. A Mr. Jefferson."

"Jefferson, eh? He's another of their leaders. What else?"

Creighton swatted irritably at a whining mosquito. "I don't know. Oh, Dr. Franklin went to a meeting of the Patriots this afternoon."

"A meeting? Where?"

"The Café. That's all they said."

"Find out what café. What else? Any sign of weapons or explosives anywhere?"

"No."

"A printing press?"

"Yes. Dr. Franklin has one. He prints the city's newspaper, the *Weekly Journal.*"

"Ah," said his uncle, as though at last Creighton had provided some information that might actually prove useful. "Does he print anything else?"

"I don't know."

"Then find out." Before Creighton could protest that he had no intention of going back to Franklin's, the colonel said, "One other thing." His voice was barely above a whisper; Creighton had to put his ear to the port to catch the words. "We mean to escape soon, before they can demand a ransom or an exchange. It should be a fairly easy matter, but we'll need your help."

"*My* help? What can *I* do?"

"Bring me a pistol."

"A pistol? Where would I— How can I—"

"I don't care where or how, just get one. The sooner the better." From within the building, Creighton heard a bolt rattle. "Go now!" his uncle said urgently, and slammed the little door into place.

Not wanting to chance being discovered by the guards, Creighton sprang up and hurried off—still with no destination in mind. He might have enough money left to stay at an inn, if he could find one, but only for a night or two, and then he'd be out on the street again.

Besides, Colonel Gower was expecting him to return to Franklin's and resume the espionage activities he had never really begun. And of course there was the matter of the pistol. Stealing one would be a risky proposition. But the only way he was likely ever to leave this godforsaken place was in the company of his uncle and Lieutenant Hale, and that meant helping them escape.

Though Dr. Franklin didn't strike him as the sort to keep guns lying about, Creighton knew of nowhere else to look.

There was nowhere else he could escape the shroud of mosquitoes that encircled him, either.

He'd never lacked courage where actual physical danger was concerned. But when he thought about having to apologize for his humiliating feat with the type form, he cringed. Still, he supposed it was better than being driven mad by the bloody mosquitoes.

Chapter TEN

Creighton hoped that Dr. Franklin might have retired by now, leaving him with only Sophie to face. But the windows in the old man's chambers were bright with candlelight. He went around to the rear of the house and slipped quietly into the pantry. No sign of Sophie. Perhaps, he thought, half guiltily and half hopefully, she was still out in the printing shop, laboriously reconstructing the hundreds of words he had destroyed in a moment of carelessness.

But as he passed through the foyer toward his room, the door to Franklin's study opened and Sophie emerged, so suddenly that Creighton nearly collided with her. She gave him a peevish look. "You are very clumsy today, *n'est-ce pas?*"

"I'm not usually." He cleared his throat uncomfortably. "Listen. About the tray of types—"

She put a finger to her lips and motioned for him to follow her to the kitchen. "The doctor has company," she explained. "Monsieur Jefferson. We must not disturb them." She set down the serving tray she had been carrying. "*Maintenant.* You were about to apologize."

"Was I?"

"Were you not?"

"I'm not much good at apologies."

"Of course not. It requires *humilité.*"

"Yes. It does. Anyway, I am . . . " He hesitated.

She nodded expectantly, waving her hands in little circles as though trying to draw the words out. "You are . . . ?"

"I'm . . . sorry that I . . . made so much work for you."

"*Très bien.* I could have set the words in type *plus rapidement* . . . more quickly than you said them, but you will improve with practice. Next week perhaps we will work on saying 'thank you.' "

Creighton laughed with something like relief. "You forgive me, then?"

She shrugged. "For the accident, yes."

"What else have I done?"

"*Rien.* Nothing. It is your people who have done it, to my people. That is more difficult to forgive."

"Do you want me to apologize for that, too?"

She smiled faintly. "*Non.* The best thing you can do is to show me that not all *Anglais* are like that."

"I'll try." The sound of some glass object shattering made him glance toward Franklin's study. "What are they doing in there?"

"*Je ne sais pas*. And I do not wish to know."

Franklin appeared in the doorway of the kitchen, holding the pieces of a broken drinking glass. "Would you pour another brandy for Mr. Jefferson, please, Sophie?" He dropped the pieces into a small dustbin and turned to Creighton. He didn't ask where Creighton had been, or why he had left; he simply said, "I'm glad you found your way back. It wasn't easy, was it?"

"No," Creighton said.

Unexpectedly, the old man gave him a broad wink. "And I dare say Mademoiselle Sophie didn't make it any easier."

Creighton glanced at Sophie, who was looking a bit indignant. "Well, she's forgiven me, at any rate."

"Good. We still need you." He took the fresh glass of brandy from Sophie. "Speaking of which, we won't be needing you any further, my dear. You may go on to bed when you like."

She frowned disapprovingly. "You will not be staying up too late, I hope?"

"No, no. Not too late." He leaned toward her and added confidentially, "Thomas is a bit gloomy this evening; he needs a sympathetic ear."

"*Je comprends*. I only worry that you will tire yourself."

He waved her concern away. "I know. But I'm as strong as an ox . . . well, an *old* ox, anyway."

When he had gone, she sighed. "He is not as strong as he would like to believe. With his gout, he should not be drinking brandy, either."

Creighton feigned astonishment. "You don't mean he's indulging in Strong Beverages?"

Sophie smiled. "Dr. Franklin does not believe in being *too* virtuous. He says that . . ." She paused and bit her lip thoughtfully, as though trying to recall the doctor's exact words. ". . . that a perfect character might be attended with the inconvenience of being envied and hated." She held up the carafe of brandy. "Would you like a little? It is not truly brandy; it is rum, which they call Barbados brandy."

"Yes . . . thank you."

"*Bon,* you are practicing already." As she poured a drink for him, her expression turned solemn. "I worry about Monsieur Jefferson, too. He mourns for his family."

"What happened to them?"

"When Monsieur Jefferson fled the Colonies with the other Patriots, he took his wife and children with him. Their *bateau* . . . their boat overturned on the Ohio River, and they were drowned." She lifted the hem of her apron and dabbed quickly at her eyes. "I think it will be difficult for him to forgive the English, too." She drew a deep breath. "*Alors. Bonsoir,* Creighton. I will see you in the morning." She started out of the kitchen, then turned back to say, "Oh, I will wash clothing tomorrow. If you will leave yours outside your door, I will do them with the others." She gave his apparel a critical glance and whispered confidentially, "They need it . . . if you do not mind my saying so."

Creighton was not accustomed to retiring so soon after dark. Back home, he had considered midnight a shockingly early bedtime. After a night's carousing, he had fallen swiftly to sleep and slept long and soundly, untroubled by the nagging thoughts and concerns that can plague a person like so many mosquitoes, making him toss and turn half the night, or lie awake staring at the ceiling.

But tonight some of what Sophie had said did nag at him, buzzing about in his brain long after he lay down. He had always thought of his countrymen as something like the standard-bearers of civilization—ambitious, perhaps even arrogant, but well intentioned, bringing prosperity and enlightenment to the less fortunate countries they colonized. He had never considered the possibility that, to the people of those countries, they might look like conquerors instead, or that British attempts to keep the peace might be seen as oppression and injustice.

Sometime in the small hours he rose from his bed to use the chamber pot. The house was still and dark, but he spied a glow of light somewhere outside. Rubbing his eyes, he went to the window and peered into the darkness. The glow was coming from beneath the door of the printing shop. Could Sophie be out there, still piecing together the ruined page of type?

Creighton searched about for his breeches, then remembered that he had left them out for Sophie to wash. Well, he wouldn't need them in the dark. He slid noiselessly through the open shutters and crept across the dewy grass to the printing shop. Since he could hardly burst in on Sophie clad only in his underclothes, he went around to the window of the log building.

The shutters were closed tightly to keep out bugs attracted to the light. He put one eye to a sizable crack between the boards. Though he couldn't make out the whole room, he could see most of the composing table, and the figure that was bent over it. It was not Sophie, but Dr. Franklin. The old man was setting type into a form—not the one Creighton had emptied so precipitously, but a smaller one, perhaps twelve inches by six. As he worked, he glanced at a paper he'd hung up on one of the type bins.

His hands were not nearly as swift and sure as Sophie's. As he was placing a lead square onto the composing stick, the piece of type slipped from his grasp and tumbled to the floor. Franklin leaned on the table and gave a heavy sigh. He rubbed at his right arm and swiveled it about as though it pained him. Wearily he pushed the tray of type aside and draped a cloth over it. After a moment's thought, he set several of the type bins atop the cloth. Then he took down the paper he had been reading from and blew out the candles that had illuminated the table. The room went black.

Creighton flattened against the logs of the building. He heard the door open and close, and heard Franklin limping up the path to the house, his gouty foot scuffing on the dirt path. Creighton wondered what sort of printing job could be so urgent—or so secret—that it had to be composed in the middle of the night. But he couldn't find out much in the dark, and he had no way of relighting the candles. It would have to wait until morning.

By the time he woke, the morning was half-gone. His breeches, shirt, coat, and waistcoat were spread out neatly across the mosquito netting. They were still a little damp, but at least they were clean.

As he walked past Franklin's room, he noticed that the door was ajar. The old man's voice came from inside. "Creighton?"

"Yes?"

"Come in a moment, will you?"

He pulled the door open warily, expecting to find the old man dressed only in nature's garb again. But Franklin had apparently done his breathing for the day, and now wore a full suit of clothing, including his fur cap. On the desk before him sat an odd apparatus no more than six inches high. It consisted of two parts: a metal ball with a small cylinder atop it and a burning candle stub beneath it, and a pivoting wooden arm that rocked up and down, driven by a thin rod that projected from inside the little cylinder. Each time the arm rose, a small jet of steam issued from the cylinder.

Franklin ignored the little machine's puffing and rocking. His attention was on the papers spread before him, which were covered with scribbles and crude sketches.

"What do you know about steam engines?" he asked abruptly.

Creighton approached the desk and examined the model. "Is that what this is?"

Franklin gave him a wry glance. "Well, I suppose that answers my question, if you don't even recognize one when you see it."

Creighton flushed angrily. "I've never spent much time in the company of machines. Perhaps you'd do better to ask a member of the working class."

Franklin seemed surprised by his tone. "Yes. Perhaps they'd have a better sense of humor." He placed a finger on one end of the wooden arm; it slowed a little, but kept rocking. "Fascinating, isn't it?"

"I suppose. It doesn't seem to actually *do* much."

"Not on this scale, no. But increase its size by a hundredfold, and imagine what it would be capable of." He leaned back in his chair. "I have heard that, thanks to the efforts of Mr. Watt, the development of the steam engine is more advanced in England than here in the Colonies. I know they're used for pumping water out of mines, and such things, but I wondered whether anything had been done in the way of powering a boat or other craft."

Creighton shook his head. "My family—" he began, and then hesitated. It might be best not to reveal much of his background. "We have acquaintances in the shipping business, and if such a thing were in use, I'm certain they would have mentioned it."

Franklin nodded and bent over his drawings and notes again. "There's no reason why it shouldn't work, really. If you were to use the arm to drive a wheel, something like a mill wheel . . ." To illustrate, he inked his quill and drew two circles side by side, then connected them with a series of short lines. "A boat equipped with a strong enough steam engine would be able to travel upriver, against the current. Instead of taking four or five months to get to the falls of the Ohio, it might take only a week or two."

"What good would that do you? That's all English territory."

Franklin smiled. "What it says on a map does not always agree with what's in the hearts of the people who live there." He waved his quill at Creighton. "Look at you, for instance."

"What about me?"

"One might call you English, too, but I doubt that's where your heart is, or you wouldn't have come here. I haven't asked why you left England, and I won't ask. That's your business. But the fact is, you did choose to leave. Now, if an individual can choose to sever his ties with his homeland, why can't a hundred people, or a thousand, or many thousands?"

Leaving England hadn't been his choice at all, of course, and he planned to return at the first opportunity. But he didn't say so. If Franklin wanted to think he had changed his loyalties, let him. And if the old man wanted to dream that the Yankeys would somehow, someday, rise again and wrest America from the hands of the British, let him.

When Franklin gathered up his papers, he revealed a booklet that had been covered by them. Creighton picked it up and perused the cover, which read:

The North American

ALMANACK

And Gentleman's and Lady's DIARY

◆◈◆

For the Year of our Lord

1777

Being the First after Bissextile, or Leap Year

Calculated for the Meridian of Richmond in Virginia but may indifferently serve any part of the Middle Colonies

CONTAINING
The Lunations, Conjunctions, Eclipses, Judgment of the Weather, Rising and Setting of the Planets, Length of Days and Nights, & c. Together with useful TABLES, Chronological OBSERVATIONS & entertaining REMARKS

"Is this something you print?" Creighton asked.

"No, no, it's printed in Virginia. I once published something similar, though, called *Poor Richard's Almanac*. Perhaps you've heard of it?"

Creighton shook his head. "Almanacs aren't much used in England, at least not among the gentry."

"No? Well, they're very popular here. I daresay that if you visited one hundred households, you'd find an almanac in at least ninety. In a good year, I used to sell fifty thousand copies of *Poor Richard's*. Perhaps I should have dubbed it *Rich Richard's* instead, eh?"

Creighton leafed through the almanac. In addition to Tables, Observations, and Remarks, it contained essays and stories, including one about settlers captured by Indians. "Do you mind if I borrow this? I'd like something to read in the evenings."

"Of course," Franklin said, but with a certain reluctance in his voice. He gestured at a small bookcase that held perhaps two dozen volumes. "Wouldn't you prefer a book, though?"

"No. This interests me. I'd like to see what people find so amusing."

"You may have it, then. But I'll want it back tomorrow so I may consult the planting tables." Franklin gazed wistfully at the bookshelf. "My library here is so meager, compared to the collection I had in Philadelphia. The shelves reached to the ceiling. I had a device like an extended fire tongs constructed, which I used to retrieve books from the highest rows." He lifted his fur hat and scratched the top of his bald head reflectively. "I wish I had even half of those volumes. But I suppose they've all been sold off by now, or burned."

"Don't you have family there who could have rescued them?"

"When the British took Philadelphia, my family were lucky to rescue themselves."

"Surely they wouldn't have been harmed? The English army is not in the habit of punishing civilians."

Franklin laughed humorlessly. "If you don't consider it a punishment to have everything you value taken from you and be reduced to poverty and near starvation, then I suppose you're right." The old man leaned forward and blew out the candle. The steam engine gave a few last puffs, then came to a halt. "Well, we have a paper to print. Let's get at it."

In the printing shop, Franklin made an impression of the page Sophie had reset and gave it to Creighton to proofread all over again. Sophie, meanwhile, began composing a second page. "No accidents this time, please," Franklin said mildly. "We need to begin printing tomorrow in order to have the *Journal* on the street by Thursday afternoon. If we're even a half hour later than usual, folk get out of sorts." He laughed. "I expect they need it to wrap Friday's fish in." He headed for the door. "I'm off to the market, now."

"That is not necessary, Doctor," Sophie said. "I will go."

He waved away her protest. "You have enough to do. Besides, the exercise will be good for my gout."

Creighton found even more errors than he had the first time around, probably because Sophie had been more rushed. Not wanting to upset her, he made small, hardly noticeable marks next to the words instead of circling them boldly.

As he worked, his gaze strayed time and again to the concealed tray of type Franklin had been setting the night before. Sophie caught him looking in her direction and gave him an inquisitive glance, as though wondering what he found so interesting. She seemed slightly flustered, too. Perhaps she imagined that she was the object of his attention. It wasn't an unreasonable assumption, actually. An essential part of being a gentleman was having an eye for a pretty face, and Sophie's, though it wasn't the sort of fair, plump countenance common among English women, was attractive in its own way.

Around noon Sophie looked up abruptly from her work and exclaimed, "*Bonté!* I nearly forgot about preparing dinner!"

Wanting to redeem himself for yesterday's disaster, Creighton said, "I'll set a few lines while you're gone, shall I?"

She gave him a startled glance. "You?"

"Yes. I'm not ordinarily so clumsy. I won't destroy anything, honestly."

Her expression softened, but was still doubtful. "Do I have your promise?"

"Upon my honor as a gentleman."

Sophie sighed. "*Eh bien. Mais prenez garde* . . . be very careful, *s'il vous plaît.*"

When she was safely in the house, Creighton removed the bins Franklin had placed atop his unfinished page of type and lifted the cloth. Though Creighton wasn't adept at reading backward, there was no mistaking what the large letters at the top of the page spelled out: THE LIBERTY TREE.

Chapter ELEVEN

he rear door of the house slammed shut, making Creighton start in alarm. He yanked the cloth back into place and stepped away from the table. But no one approached the printing shop. Perhaps Sophie had only been tossing dishwater or scraps out the door.

Creighton took up the ink and the roller and quickly spread a film of ink on the type. Then he laid down a blank sheet of paper, and with a clean roller, pressed it against the type. When he peeled the paper away, it bore an impression of the page that was, if not flawless, at least readable.

He wiped the type clean, covered it, and placed the wooden bins on it. When the printed page had dried, he folded it into a small square and tucked it into the pocket of his waistcoat. His uncle would be pleased to learn that he had discovered the source of the rebels' propaganda. Creighton was rather pleased, too, that he had proven himself so adept at spying.

But at the same time he felt a strange and unexpected twinge of something like regret . . . or was it guilt? He'd experienced regret often enough—for example, when he'd foolishly bet money he didn't have on a winning hand of cards he didn't have. But he wasn't quite so familiar with guilt.

What his mother called his "wild behavior" had never bothered his conscience much. Neither had his failure to excel at school, or the times he'd taken money or valuables from his mother. Why, then, should his conscience choose to trouble him now?

The fact that Franklin had taken him in and trusted him and treated him with kindness didn't mean he owed the old man any sort of loyalty. It would take far more than a little kindness to make him forget that it was Franklin's countrymen who had killed his father. Besides, he wasn't deliberately trying to harm Franklin; he was only doing his uncle's bidding so the colonel wouldn't leave him behind.

To calm his conscience further, he set about correcting the mistakes Sophie had made when she reassembled the page he had disassembled. It was harder than it looked, locating one misspelled word among all the others and then selecting the proper letters from the bins. He had redone only five or six words before Sophie appeared to summon him to dinner.

When she saw him bent over the completed page and not the new one, she frowned. "You do not need to correct my errors, Creighton. I will do it."

"I just thought I'd save you the trouble." He wiped his brow. "It's not easy."

She came up next to him and glanced at the paper he had proofread. "You did not circle the words that were wrong?"

"No. I just—"

"I see. You made little marks." She scanned the columns of print and grimaced. *"Dieu!"* she said softly. "So many mistakes!" She shoved the paper aside in disgust. "I never made so many before. Before—" She broke off.

"Before I came?" Creighton finished. "I'm sorry, but I don't make them, I only find them. It's not my fault if you can't read properly."

She glared at him. "I read *le français* well enough. And I am working at English, with Dr. Franklin's *assistance*. As I say, it is a stupid language."

"A stupid language," Creighton said simultaneously. "I know. But if you can't read it, how do you—I mean, how can you possibly—" He waved a hand at the thousands of backward letters and punctuation marks that filled the forms and the bins.

She shrugged. "It is not so very *difficile*. Though I may not know most of the words, I know what the letters look like, and where to find them."

"But how do you do it so quickly?"

Sophie lifted her chin haughtily. "I suppose I am just naturally *douée* . . . gifted."

"And so modest, too."

She blinked at him innocently, but with a hint of mischief in her eyes. "Maw-dest? I am afraid I have not yet learned that word."

Creighton grinned. "That's odd, considering that, in French, the word is exactly the same."

"*Non,* it is not," she said primly. "Ours has an *e* on the end."

"And so," Creighton reminded her, "does *humilité.*"

125

She winced and hung her head, like a schoolgirl who has forgotten to study her lessons. "*Eh bien.* There are some things at which I am not so naturally gifted. However," she added brightly, "cooking is not one of them. So come and eat."

Before Creighton retired to his room that evening, he asked Sophie for a candle to read by. He didn't bother to mention what he'd be reading.

Most of the half-completed page of *The Liberty Tree* was occupied by an essay that urged inhabitants of Kentucky and the western territories of America to secede, ally themselves with Spain, and form a new nation free from British rule.

The author of the essay wasn't identified. At the end of the piece was the word *Anonymous,* followed by the number 29. Creighton doubted that Franklin had written it; the tone was too strident, too humorless.

At the top of the second column of type were more numbers, a long sequence of them that went on for five lines. They were divided into clumps, like words, usually four or five numerals to a clump, but occasionally three or six. Creighton recognized it at once as a code of some kind.

Before he and his schoolmates took to playing Hangman so avidly, they had been equally enthusiastic about codes and ciphers. They had exchanged scores of secret messages that, written in the usual fashion, would have been hopelessly ordinary and inconsequential. But because they were written in vinegar and could be read only by holding the paper over a candle flame, they seemed mysterious and exotic.

Creighton knew his uncle would want a look at the paper as soon as possible, but he couldn't resist the challenge of trying to decipher it. Besides, wouldn't the page be more valuable once it was translated?

There were half a dozen common keys that might unlock the secret of the code. He started with the simplest: Each numeral stood for a letter of the alphabet—1 for *A,* 2 for *B,* and so on. When he applied this formula, printing the letters lightly with a pencil, the first three words proved to be *MRYG, PUPAH,* and *SHVEN.* Interesting, but not very informative. They might be words from some obscure language, but that didn't seem likely. He was sure that most Americans had trouble enough reading English, let alone Sanskrit or Prussian.

He tried again. Perhaps the matching of numbers and letters wasn't so obvious and orderly. The most commonly used letter was *E,* and the number that appeared most often in the message was 4, so he replaced every 4 with an *E.* One of the three-number clumps, 724, now ended with an *E*—probably the word *THE.* That meant every 7 was a *T,* and every 2 was an *H.* But when he penciled these in, he ended up with one word that was spelled *EHHH.* The word *eh?* pronounced with a Yankey drawl, perhaps? No. He wiped out his efforts with a piece of India rubber and started over.

After two hours of failed attempts, Creighton flung the paper aside in frustration and sank back on the bed, rubbing his weary eyes. Who would have thought the backward Yankeys could come up with a system that was so difficult to decipher? It must have been Dr. Franklin's doing.

He was about to give up and blow out the candle when he remembered another sort of code he and his schoolmates had once used. Most of the boys had tired of the whole business after a week or so. But Creighton and two other boys, inspired by the romantic exploits of a French footman who had been hanged for stealing state secrets, devised a more sophisticated—and deliciously sacrilegious—method of sending coded messages, using the Holy Bible as the key. For example, the cipher G43193 meant Book of Genesis, chapter 43, verse 19, word 3. It was a cumbersome system, but it had the advantage of using a book that could be found almost anywhere. They tried just citing a particular page and line, but that wasn't reliable; there were too many different editions of the Bible.

Then one Sunday during Bible study, the pastor intercepted a message that concerned the neckline of a certain young lady's dress. Threatening the note's author with hellfire, the pastor pried from him the details of the code. Their experiments came to an abrupt end.

The clumps of numerals in Franklin's message might refer to page, line, and word—but of what book? It had to be something that would be found in nearly every household . . .

Creighton sat up in bed. On his nightstand, next to the candle, lay the almanac he had borrowed from Franklin.

He raised the mosquito netting, snatched the booklet, and let the netting drop so quickly that no more than ten or twelve mosquitoes invaded his sanctum.

The first cipher on the paper was 1143. Creighton turned to page one of the almanac. It was a calendar for the month of January, with brief weather predictions. Line one didn't contain forty-three words. On line fourteen there were no words, only astrological symbols. He tried page eleven, line four, word three: *ALL*. He sighed with satisfaction. At last, an actual, sensible word. Creighton penciled it in and eagerly tracked down the next word: *ATTEMPTS*.

Certain that he had the key now, he raced on. The process went much faster once he discovered that, in clumps of three or more numerals, the first two always represented the page number. In no more than a quarter hour, he had translated the entire message—with the exception of one word:

ALL ATTEMPTS BY SONS OF LIBERTY TO LEARN WHERE
_____ IS BEING HELD HAVE BEEN UNSUCCESSFUL IF ANY
PERSON HAS INFORMATION ON THIS MATTER PLEASE
DIRECT A MESSAGE IN CODE TO CAFÉ OF EXILES NEW
ORLEANS

The one cipher he couldn't solve contained just two nu-merals—a 4 and a 6. It couldn't denote page, line, and word. It must be a code within the code, a number used in place of someone's name. That would also explain the two-digit number that appeared after the word *Anonymous*.

There was no way of knowing what number signified what member of the self-styled Sons of Liberty. But that was a small matter. The important thing was, he'd successfully broken the Yankeys' code—which meant that no message they sent from now on would be secret.

Creighton smiled smugly. His uncle had had the gall to call him useless and incompetent. Well, he'd make the man eat his words. The smile turned into a yawn. Wearily, he folded up the paper, returned it to his waistcoat pocket, and blew out the candle. His uncle could wait until tomorrow.

As he lay there in the dark, Creighton felt his sense of triumph slowly slipping away, and he realized that there was another secret, cryptic message he would have to examine and decipher the meaning of; it was coming from his conscience. He shook his head as though to clear it. His conscience, too, would have to wait.

In his dreams he and Sophie were being pursued by wild Indians. Though Indians were said to move soundlessly through the woods, these must belong to some particularly clumsy tribe, for Creighton could hear them pounding along only a few yards behind him. Sophie had evidently turned her ankle; she was limping badly and calling "Doctor! My ankle! Doctor! My ankle!"

Just before the Indians caught them, Creighton woke, gasping and drenched with sweat. The room was dark. From out in the foyer he heard the pounding that he had mistaken for footfalls, and a voice shouting "Dr. Franklin! Dr. Franklin!"

Groping about in the dark, he located his breeches and pulled them on. Then he opened his door and peered into the foyer. Someone was beating on the door to Dr. Franklin's chambers. From the size of the figure, Creighton guessed it was Peter. "What's wrong?" Creighton demanded groggily.

Peter turned toward him. "I need Dr. Franklin's help, but I can't seem to raise him!" Just then the door swung open. The old man poked out his nightcap-clad head and was very nearly knocked senseless by Peter's huge fist. "Dr. Franklin! You need to come at once!"

Franklin yawned and held up one hand. "Just a moment." He removed a lump of what looked like candle wax from each of his ears. "That's better. Now, what is it?"

"It's General Arnold!" Peter replied frantically. "He's gotten himself into a duel!"

<hr/>

Chapter TWELVE

Creighton noticed for the first time that Peter was brandishing a flintlock pistol. Dr. Franklin put a hand on the giant's arm. "Calm down now and tell me where and when."

Peter took a deep breath. "St. Anthony's Square! At dawn!"

Franklin glanced through the open door at the sky, which was growing gray around the edges. "Dawn isn't far off. Luckily, neither is St. Anthony's." He eyed the pistol. "What do you intend to do with that?"

Peter looked at the weapon as though he'd just realized he had it. "It's General Arnold's—for the duel. He's asked me to be his second."

"Is it loaded?"

"Of course."

"Well, put it away. Guns make me uneasy."

Peter stuck the pistol into the rear of his waistband.

"I'll just put some clothing on," Franklin said.

"Hurry, please." The giant turned to Creighton. "Can you come, too? We might need your help."

"My help? To do what?"

"Why, to stop the tarnal duel!"

"You can't *stop* a duel. It's a matter of honor. Besides, hardly anyone ever gets killed. It's not really a fight so much as it is a formality, a sort of game."

Peter shook his head. "Not to General Arnold, it an't. He won't be satisfied till one of 'em is dead."

"Then how do you propose to stop him?"

"I don't know," Peter said grimly.

To Creighton, duels were much like hangings: though he didn't much care to participate in one, they inspired in him a certain morbid fascination, a desire to see how the gentlemen involved would conduct themselves. He pulled on his shirt and shoes and emerged from his room just as Peter and Franklin were departing.

"Gad, I hope we an't too late," Peter said.

"Well," observed Dr. Franklin, "if you've got the pistol, they're not likely to start without you."

"They might use swords. The other fellow is a fencing master."

"Good heavens," said Franklin, and limped along a little faster. "Arnold is a brave fellow, but he's no swordsman."

By the time they reached St. Anthony's Square, the edge of the sun was just showing over the horizon. The place was nothing like the main square of the city, only a small grassy field surrounded by trees and shrubs, almost invisible from the street. When they entered the clearing, only one man stood there, looking about impatiently. It was Arnold.

He scowled when he spotted the three of them. "I only wanted a second, Peter, not a third and fourth."

"I—I just thought—" Peter stammered.

"He fetched me to try to talk some sense into you," Franklin said. "Where's your opponent?"

"Late," said Arnold. "Frenchies are late for everything; it's in their blood."

"Oh, don't make such sweeping generalizations. And don't tell me about the French. I've lived among them, and I know that every one is different, just as every American is different. Now, what's this about?"

"He called me a *mauvais Kaintock*. I replied that he was a scurvy Papist, and I knocked him down."

"Hmm. Fisticuffs. That's a grave insult."

"So is calling me a Kaintock."

"What's a Kaintock?" Creighton whispered to Peter.

"A body from Kentucky. The French use it to mean you're crude and vulgar. I've heard that when French youngsters act up, their folks tell 'em the Kaintocks will get 'em."

Franklin placed a calming hand on Arnold's shoulder. "I understand that you're angry about this. But think about what you're doing. You know the governor's made dueling illegal, and we can't afford to antagonize him. Our position here is precarious enough as it is. Besides, we need the Spanish on our side."

"Yes, but, damnation, Doctor, that doesn't mean we have to swallow their insults!"

Franklin sighed, lifted the fur hat, and scratched the top of his head. "I hate disputes. There are so many pressing things that need doing in the world, and so little time to do them, it seems a pity to waste one's energy on quarreling."

"How can he say that?" Creighton whispered. "He's just finished a war with England."

"He was never in favor of a fight," Peter replied. "He did his best to settle things peacefully."

This was news to Creighton. For much of his life he'd heard and believed that Yankeys were warmongers, that they'd sent Franklin to England only to present their unreasonable demands to the king. He'd never imagined that a representative of the Colonies would make a plea for peace.

As the sun began to show through the trees, two more men came into view, strolling casually across the clearing. Arnold stiffened and turned to Peter. "Where is the pistol?"

Peter reached for it, but Franklin stayed him. "Wait. Let me talk to them. Don't worry, I won't do anything to damage your honor." Before Arnold could protest, the old man was limping across the field to intercept the Frenchman and his second.

While Arnold stood scowling, Franklin and the fencing master carried on a spirited discussion, with much hand waving on both sides. Creighton couldn't hear a word of it, but it scarcely mattered; it was probably all in French anyway.

After several minutes, the Frenchman abruptly nodded. He turned toward Arnold and gave a brief but graceful bow. Then he strode off with his second close behind. Franklin rejoined the others, looking pleased with himself.

"What did you say to him?" Arnold demanded.

Franklin shrugged. "Oh, nothing much. I simply reminded him . . . politely, of course—the French set great store by *politesse*—that, as a former ambassador to France, I was a close personal friend of His Royal Majesty, Louis the Sixteenth, and assured him that, if he didn't behave himself, I would see to it that he was condemned as a traitor and banished from his homeland forever."

Arnold stared at him a moment. "Oh," he said finally.

Franklin yawned. "Now that that's settled, I, for one, am going back to bed."

"I'll walk a ways with you," Arnold said. "There's something I'd like to discuss."

As the two men walked off, Peter said, "I'm hungry as a horse. Will you join me for some breakfast?"

Creighton didn't often rise early enough for a meal that could be called breakfast. He wasn't all that eager for the giant's company, either. But it occurred to him that there was one compelling reason to accept the invitation. "All right."

Peter seemed so pleased that it made Creighton feel a little ashamed. As they emerged from the bushes and onto the street, the giant said, "I don't ever have much chance to make friends with fellows my own age. There an't many here, except for Creoles, and they an't very well-disposed towards us."

"I've noticed. Why is that?"

"I believe they're worried that we're going to make trouble for 'em. They think the Brits—sorry, the *English*—might attack the city so as to flush us out."

"Do you suppose that's likely?"

Peter shrugged. "I can't say. I know it'd be a risky thing to do; it'd be like declaring war on France and Spain both."

They came to a spot where the edge of the dirt street had been undermined by water coursing down the drainage ditch. When Creighton stepped on the soft earth, his foot went out from under him, and with a cry of dismay, he fell to one knee.

Peter rushed to his aid. "Faith! Are you hurt?"

"I don't think so. Could you help me up?"

The giant bent down, placed his huge hands under Creighton's arms, and hauled him effortlessly to his feet.

"Thanks." Creighton put his weight on the foot that had slipped and grimaced. "I think I twisted it."

"Lean on me," Peter said. "There's a tavern just down the street. You can sit there and rest."

By the time they reached the tavern, Creighton was walking normally again. "I can manage on my own now."

"That's topping. Come on inside, then, and have something to eat. I'm buying."

"No, no, you go ahead. I just thought of something I have to do . . . for Dr. Franklin."

Peter's disappointment was obvious. "Can't it wait awhile?"

"No. It's for the paper. It has to be done this morning."

"Oh. Well. You're sure you can walk that far all right?"

"Yes, yes, I'm fine," Creighton said, a bit irritated by the giant's solicitousness. When he saw the hurt in Peter's face, he said, with some effort, "Thanks for your help."

Peter nodded. "I'll see you later on, then?"

"Yes. Later." As soon as Peter disappeared into the tavern, Creighton hurried back up the street until he reached the spot where he had stumbled. He crouched down, spread apart the reeds that choked the ditch, and retrieved the pistol he had deliberately dislodged from Peter's waist-band.

It would be best to deliver the pistol to his uncle after dark. In the meantime, Creighton concealed it beneath his bed.

That afternoon, they began printing the *Journal*. Franklin assumed the task of inking the type and placing the sheets of paper atop it; Creighton slid the form into place on the press and worked the lever; Sophie hung the printed pages on lines strung across the room and, once they were dry, folded and stacked them.

As the new member of the team, Creighton felt inept and clumsy at first, but before long he began to relax and fell into a sort of rhythm. He learned where to stand so that Franklin didn't ink him as well as the type, when to slide the form into place so that it didn't take Franklin's fingers with it, how to peel off the paper without tearing it, and how to pass it swiftly to Sophie without dropping it or colliding with her.

The precise timing and the intricate steps put Creighton in mind of the minuets and contradances performed by guests at the elegant balls back home. But the snatches of conversation that accompanied them were rather different. At a ball, most of what was said was either flattery, flirta-tion, or gossip. Here the talk was of a more mundane, practical nature, but there was a certain amount of good-natured banter, too.

Creighton had never thought he could find pleasure in anything that resembled work, but he found that there was something oddly satisfying in filling a blank sheet of paper with words, in watching the pile of printed sheets grow, in knowing that he was, if not an essential part, at least a useful part, of the process. When Dr. Franklin measured the stack of folded papers and announced, "We're nearly halfway there! Excellent work, my friends!" it was more gratifying than a hundred of the empty compliments that circulated, like counterfeit money, throughout Bristol society.

Late in the day Peter turned up and asked to speak to Creighton—privately. Creighton hoped that Franklin would say he couldn't be spared, for he suspected what was on Peter's mind. But the doctor said cheerfully, "Yes, go on. I can use a rest, anyway. My arms feel like sausages."

"I will bring us some *rafraîchissements,*" Sophie said.

Creighton reluctantly stepped outside. Peter wasted no time in stating his business. "I did something stupid," he said. "I lost General Arnold's pistol."

Creighton feigned surprise. "Oh? That's too bad. But why tell me about it?"

The giant shifted about uncomfortably. "Because, I thought . . ." Creighton feared that an accusation was coming. Instead Peter said, "I thought maybe you'd remember what I did with it. I stuck it in my waistband, I know that much, but after that . . . Hang it, I just don't remember." He struck his forehead with one huge hand, as though to punish his stubborn brain. "I'm such a blockhead some-times."

"Could you have left it at the tavern?" Creighton sug-gested. "Someone might have made off with it."

"Maybe." The giant shook his head mournfully. "General Arnold is going to be so angry at me. That was his best pistol."

"I'm sorry." Creighton's regret was painfully genuine. "I wish I could help you."

Peter smiled feebly. "That's all right. It an't your fault." He sighed. "I guess I'll have to go and tell him. Thank you."

As he slouched off, Creighton called after him, "Good luck," and the giant raised a hand halfheartedly in ac-knowledgment.

After refreshments, the three returned to their tasks. But this time Creighton was so distracted that he stepped on Sophie's foot, dropped a printed sheet, and pinched Franklin's hand in the press—not severely, but enough to elicit an uncharacteristic curse from the old man, who then felt it necessary to apologize to Sophie for his crude language.

Sophie dismissed it with a laugh. "*C'est rien.* I do not know the meaning of that word you used, anyway."

Creighton was so sick of having to apologize for things that he sullenly refused to say he was sorry. For the rest of the afternoon, those unspoken words seemed to hang in the hot, humid air of the shop, making it even more un-comfortable. Creighton was glad when Franklin measured the pile of papers and informed them that they had reached the requisite five hundred copies, half a day ahead of schedule. "Well done," he said, beaming. "Both of you."

With appropriate humility, Sophie smiled and curtsied. Creighton busied himself with washing the type and pretended he hadn't heard. What did it matter, anyway, whether he did the job well or poorly? In a day, or perhaps two—as soon as his uncle and Lieutenant Hale had completed their escape plans—he'd be gone.

Chapter THIRTEEN

That night he went to bed fully clothed and lay awake, waiting for the house to grow quiet and for the streets of the city to become deserted. Finally he rose, fished the pistol from beneath the bed, and slipped as soundlessly as any Indian out the window of his room, resisting the impulse to swat at the mosquitoes, which had no trouble locating him, no matter how silently he moved.

He made his way through the dark streets as quickly as he could and approached the Cabildo from the rear. The only light came from the room where the guards were posted. Creighton drew out the pistol and, reaching into one of the rifle ports, rapped the end of the barrel against the wooden hatch. There was no reply from inside. He pounded harder, hoping the noise wouldn't bring the guards down upon him. Finally the little door swung open, and a soft voice said, "Creighton?"

"Hale? I've got the pistol."

"Good lad! Pass it to me."

Creighton thrust the gun forward and felt Hale take hold of the barrel. But the lieutenant seemed unable to pull it through. Creighton heard metal scrape against brick and mortar, then heard Hale growl, "Odd's death! It won't go! The port's too small!"

Creighton took hold of the pistol's grip again and pushed. "No!" the lieutenant protested. "Don't try to force it!" Abruptly Creighton jerked the weapon back. There was an explosion, and the pistol jumped in Creighton's hand. He heard a grunt of surprise or pain or both from Hale, followed a second later by someone shouting in Spanish.

It took Creighton a moment to grasp what had happened: When he attempted to push the gun through, the hammer had caught on the rough mortar and half cocked itself. Then, when he pulled it back, the hammer had released, struck a spark, and set off the powder.

From within the room came a succession of sounds: a hollow thump; more cries and curses, both in Spanish and in English; frantic scuffling noises. Creighton guessed that the guards had opened the door and were trying to subdue the prisoners.

With the pistol in his hand, Creighton dashed around the building and burst through the front door. In the light from a pair of candles, he could make out the form of a guard standing in the doorway of the prisoners' quarters, pointing his musket at two men on the floor, locked in a desperate struggle. Hale stood slumped against the rear wall, holding his arm.

Creighton sprang forward, flung one arm around the neck of the guard with the musket, and pressed the pistol to the man's temple. "Drop it! Drop the gun!"

Whether or not the man understood English, he got the message. "*Sí, sí!*" he cried, his voice choked. He uncocked the hammer and, with Creighton still clinging to his neck, crouched carefully and laid the musket on the floor.

Hale approached the two struggling men and delivered a swift kick to the second guard's ribs. The man curled into a ball, groaning and clutching his belly.

Colonel Gower rose unsteadily, dusted himself off, and wiped blood from one corner of his mouth. "Find something to tie up these two."

Hale pushed past Creighton and his captive. "That was quick thinking," he said. "I only wish you hadn't shot me."

"Sorry. Is it bad?"

The lieutenant shrugged, and then winced. "I'll live." He cut the rawhide thongs off the guards' hats. "Sit down, señor," he told the guard who was still in Creighton's grip. He bound the guard's wrists together, tied them to the man's ankles, then gagged the man's mouth with a cloth. Creighton's throat tightened in sympathy as he remembered how it felt. Hale trussed up the other guard in the same fashion, then locked both men in the room he and the colonel had just occupied.

Gower, meanwhile, had picked up the men's muskets and taken their powder horns and shot bags off the wall. He approached Creighton and held out a hand. Thinking his uncle meant to express his thanks, Creighton stuck the pistol in his waistband and extended his own hand. The colonel glanced at it, then reached out and took the pistol. "Well, for all his faults, your father was no coward. It appears that you take after him in that respect."

Hale surveyed the street outside. "It's all clear, sir; we'd best go."

"In a moment." The colonel turned back to Creighton. "Have you learned anything more of any value?"

Creighton fished the page of *The Liberty Tree* from his waistcoat and handed it to him. The colonel unfolded it and held it close to the candle. "Excellent." He thrust the paper into his pocket. "See what else you can find out."

"What else? What do you mean? I'm going with you."

Gower shook his head. "You're of more use to me here. If you came with us, you'd only slow us down."

Hale gave the colonel a look of surprise. "Surely, sir, the boy deserves—"

Gower raised a hand to cut him off. "He will remain here. Those are my orders."

"You can't give me orders!" Creighton cried. "I'm not a soldier! I'm coming with you!"

The colonel's only reply was a hard, warning glance. He turned and strode from the room.

"I'm sorry, lad," Hale said softly, and followed.

For a moment Creighton stood there, dumbfounded. Then he ran outside and seized the colonel's arm. "You can't leave me—" he started to protest.

Gower yanked his arm free, raised the pistol, and brought the barrel down hard on top of his nephew's head. Creighton crumpled to the ground, dazed, unable to move, unable to think, unable to see anything except a sort of dark haze all around, into which two slightly darker shadows were blending, disappearing.

He had no idea how long he lay there, on the cusp of consciousness, before he heard the guards begin pounding on the door of their cell and calling for help. At first Creighton was glad; whoever came to their aid could help him, too. But some other part of his brain said that if he was discovered here, it would be obvious that he'd helped the English prisoners escape; the two guards would identify him.

He tried to get to his feet and nearly passed out. Even crawling on hands and knees was an effort. Though it sent pain shooting through his skull, he managed to shuffle around the end of the building, where he wouldn't be seen. After a minute's rest, he grabbed hold of a small tree and pulled himself upright a few inches at a time. He leaned against the trunk for another minute or two, until he heard voices and the rattle of muskets coming from the watch house. Then he forced himself to move.

In the past, when he'd been ill or injured, he'd been well looked after. His mother had put him to bed at once, summoned a doctor, and instructed a maid to see to his every need. It was all so gratifying that he had sometimes invented or exaggerated some complaint just so he could lie abed for a few days and be pampered. Now here he was, in worse distress than ever before in his life, and there was no one to care for him. He didn't even have a home to go to. He had to go somewhere, though, before the city watch stumbled upon him, and there was nowhere to go but Dr. Franklin's house—though he wasn't at all sure he could reach it or, in his confused state, even find it.

Later on, he would recall his passage through the dark streets the way one recalls a nightmare. His feet seemed rooted to the ground; each step was a struggle. He had no clear sense of where he was or where he was going; he only staggered on and on endlessly, through a vague, featureless landscape, trusting that, at some point, he would wake and find himself safe in his bed.

When he did finally become fully conscious again, he was indeed in bed. For a delirious moment he convinced himself that he was home and that all the misery he had been through, from the abduction to his uncle's betraying and deserting him, had been part of a fevered dream, brought on by some illness that had left his head hurting unmercifully and his face hot and swollen.

Then he opened his eyes and saw the mosquito netting draped over him like a shroud, and he knew that he had dreamed none of it. He squeezed his eyelids shut again, so hard and so long that tears seeped from beneath them.

There was a soft rapping on his door, and Sophie's anxious voice. "Creighton? *Vas-tu bien?* Are you all right?"

Creighton wasn't sure how to answer. With the truth? That he was as badly off as he could possibly be, short of being captured by Indians or being up to his neck in quicksand? No, she'd only ask why. It was better to lie.

"Creighton?" she called again.

It took him a moment to get his voice working, and even then it sounded feeble and hoarse. "I think I'm ill."

"Ah, *c'est dommage.* May I come in?"

"No!" Creighton replied, so vehemently that it sent a stab of pain through his aching head. "I'm . . . I'm not dressed." Another lie. He was fully clothed, but his clothing was streaked with dirt and dried blood. That would be hard to explain. So would the blood-caked lump on top of his head, and the mosquito bites that had ravaged his unprotected face.

"Shall I send for *le médecin* . . . the doctor?"

"No! No. It's nothing serious, I'm sure. If I could just rest for a while . . ."

"*Mais, oui.* I will bring you some tea or some bouillon later on, then."

Creighton smiled faintly. It was a little like being home, at least. "Yes. That would be nice."

Though it set his head pounding, he dragged himself to the washstand, where he gingerly rinsed most of the dried blood from his hair and scrubbed some of the dirt from the knees of his breeches. Then, exhausted, he lay down and covered himself with the linen sheet.

Not long afterward the door to his room opened. He turned his head painfully, expecting to see Sophie bearing a tea tray. It was Dr. Franklin. "Sophie tells me you're not feeling well. I thought I'd look in on you."

"It's nothing much," Creighton said weakly. "Probably just a touch of ague."

"Perhaps, but we need to be sure it's not the yellow fever." He bent and, putting on his split-lensed spectacles, peered at Creighton's face. "Why, you're covered with bites, my boy. Is there a hole in your netting?"

"No. I probably just knocked it aside, tossing and turning."

"Hmm." He removed the glasses and tucked them into his waistcoat pocket. "And is that how you came by the gash on your head, as well?"

Creighton averted his eyes from the old man's penetrating gaze. "No," he said, but his brain was too muddled to concoct a reasonable explanation.

Franklin pulled up a chair next to the bed and sat down. Creighton tensed, expecting questions, accusations. Instead, the old man said casually, "You know, it's too bad we got the paper printed up so quickly. I've just learned some news that would have made a compelling story. Now, unless we print up a special edition, it will have to wait until next week." He leaned back in the chair and folded his hands over his belly. "Would you like to know what the news was?"

Though Creighton suspected he already knew, he swallowed to ease the tightness in his throat and said, "All right."

"It seems that the two English prisoners made their escape from the Cabildo late last night, aided by a third person."

"Oh?" Creighton said as nonchalantly as he could. "Have they been caught?"

"No. The authorities believe they stole a boat and made their way downriver." He paused. "All three of them, apparently."

"Well," Creighton said. "That's good."

Franklin's eyebrows went up. "Good? How so?"

"I was indentured to the colonel, remember. I can't say I'm sorry to be rid of him."

"No, I suppose not. Unfortunately we had hoped to exchange him and the lieutenant for some of our own captured officers. So, as you may imagine, we Patriots are not so happy about losing them. General Arnold is particularly upset. If he were to catch any of the three, it would go hard with them."

Creighton swallowed hard again. "Is there any chance of that?"

Franklin drummed his fingers together thoughtfully. "I'd say that depends."

"On what?"

The doctor leaned forward. "On what you have to tell me, and whether or not I believe it."

Creighton considered denying any part in the escape and any knowledge of it. But there was little chance that

149

he could fool the shrewd old man, even for a moment. His only hope was to tell the truth—or something close to it. He held his throbbing head with both hands and sighed. "I helped them escape."

"I know that. What I'd like to know is why. You seem to have no fondness for your former master. Why help him?"

"I didn't do it for him. I did it for Lieutenant Hale. He was my friend."

"I see." Franklin examined Creighton's skull. "And the ostrich egg on your head?"

Creighton was ready with a plausible answer. "The colonel tried to force me to go with him. When I resisted, he struck me."

"And then left you behind?"

"I believe he thought he'd killed me." Creighton ruefully fingered the lump. "I thought he had, too, for a time."

"You're lucky he didn't. A blow to the head is nothing to sneeze at." He regarded Creighton long and thoughtfully. "I've heard that it can damage a person's memory. It hasn't done that to you, has it?"

"No," Creighton said.

"Then everything you've told me is true?"

"On my honor."

This reply seemed to satisfy the old man. He pushed back his chair and rose. "I don't see that anyone else needs to know about this," he said. Then he shook a warning finger at Creighton. "One thing, though."

"What's that?"

"I wouldn't go anywhere where you're likely to encounter those two guards."

"Does that mean you don't want me to interview them for your newspaper?"

Franklin laughed. "I think not. In fact, I don't want you doing much of anything for a day or two, except resting. When you feel up to reading a book, let me know and I'll bring you some."

"Thank you," Creighton said. "And not just for the books."

The old man took a moment to reply, as though he were weighing Creighton's words. Finally he said, "Yes, well, I've given you a lot of rope, you know. See that you don't hang yourself with it."

Chapter FOURTEEN

*P*ampering was apparently one of those words Sophie didn't quite grasp the meaning of. Instead of the licorice tea and biscuits Creighton had come to expect when he was ill, she brought him a pot of vile-tasting stuff—green tea, she told him, with a dose of powdered willow bark to ease the pain in his head. She seemed to be under the impression that he had fainted and struck his head on the washstand. Creighton smiled to himself; clearly Franklin was no slouch at lying, either, when the occasion called for it.

Even after he added several spoonfuls of honey, the tea was difficult to get down. When he complained, Sophie replied, not very sympathetically, "*Eh bien,* life is like that, *n'est-ce pas?* Without suffering, there is no improvement." There was little doubt about where she'd come by that bit of wisdom.

"I was already suffering," Creighton pointed out grumpily. But he had to admit that the potion did make his head hurt less. He wasn't ready to start slinging type forms around anytime soon, however. "What about the newspaper? Don't we need to distribute it?"

"Oh, *non,* that's taken care of. We have a *troupe* of creole boys who sell them on the corners of the streets."

The thought of several hundred people poring over and discussing something he had helped to print gave Creighton an unfamiliar sense of satisfaction. Though he had never considered taking up a trade of any sort, aside from gambling, he could almost imagine himself being a printer.

That evening Dr. Franklin appeared with a copy of *Roderick Random* and read aloud from it, by the light of a myrtleberry candle, for nearly an hour. Sophie declared that she had trouble taking in so many English words at once, but she stood in the doorway for a long time, listening. It was a far cry from the raucous evenings Creighton had spent in taverns with his rakish companions, and yet he was sorry when the old man yawned, closed the book, and bid him good night.

The following morning, Peter stopped in to see how he was faring. Franklin had obviously told him the same lie he'd told Sophie, for the giant crouched and examined the base of the washstand.

"What are you looking for?" Creighton demanded.

"Oh, nothing. It's just that, if it'd been *my* head, it would have broke the washstand. I guess yours an't as hard." He stood and produced a deck of cards from his pocket. "I thought you might be bored, and I've heard you're fond of cards."

Creighton grinned and arranged his pillows so he could sit upright. "I am indeed."

Peter lowered his huge frame onto the chair carefully, as though afraid it might collapse under him. "Dr. Franklin thought you might like chess better, but I'm no good at that. It makes my head hurt."

"I didn't suppose that you Yankeys would be fond of such a complex game."

Peter kept his eyes on the deck of cards he was shuffling. "You don't think much of Americans, do you?"

It would have taken too much effort to lie. "No."

"Pardon me if I sound rude, but why did you come here, then?" Creighton didn't answer. "Dr. Franklin says he thinks maybe your family disowned you. Is that it?"

"Something like that."

"You've no call to be ashamed. To tell the truth, that's the very reason my father had to leave. Him and my grandfather quarreled, and he knocked the old man sense-less with a whiffletree."

Creighton stifled a laugh, and put a hand to his aching head. "I'm sorry. I guess it's not really very funny. So your father was born in England?"

"Half the Americans you meet was born there." He dealt a hand of cards to each of them. "See here, when you're feeling better, why don't I take you to the Café and intro-duce you around. You could have a drink with the fellows, and maybe play a few hands of cards. What do you say?"

Disagreeing would have required too much effort, too. "All right," Creighton said, just so Peter would drop the subject.

They spent a reasonably pleasant hour or two playing commerce. Peter was not the sort of companion Creighton would have chosen if he'd had a choice, but the giant was amiable enough. Besides, Creighton would probably have welcomed any company at all. It kept him from having to think about his uncle.

He had tried to tell himself that the colonel was right, that his presence would only have made the escape more risky and difficult. He had even half convinced himself that once the men reached English territory, Gower would send someone to rescue him. But some things can be seen most clearly in the darkest hours of the night, and as he lay awake that night, Creighton found he could lie to him-self no longer. If he ever hoped to escape from Louisiana, he'd have to do it on his own.

By his third day of idleness, Creighton had his fill of it. When Dr. Franklin asked if he was up to a bit of proofreading, he readily agreed. He wished now that he hadn't also agreed to join Peter and his friends at the Café. They were sure to prove insufferably dull compared with his card-playing companions back home. But he still felt indebted to Peter for having gotten him in trouble over the lost pistol. So when the giant came to fetch him, he reluctantly let himself be taken off to the Café des Exiles.

In England, the image of the typical Yankey was much like the French image of the Kaintock—an unlettered, uncivilized lout who, though really not much account as a fighter, was far better at fighting than at thinking. Franklin had proven that not all rebels fit that mold. Still, Creighton had supposed that the old man was just some rare exception to the rule.

Though most of the Patriots he met that evening wouldn't have fit in very well at a society soirée in England, they were far from being backwoods buffoons. Before the war, a number of them had been wealthy landowners in Virginia or Maryland or the Carolinas; others had been prosperous merchants in Boston or Philadelphia. Several had been educated at Oxford or had sent their sons there. A few had actually lived much of their lives in Britain; one of these, a fellow named Tom Paine, had been in America only three years.

Like Creighton's old companions, these men were fond of ale and cigars. According to Paine, the clouds of smoke discouraged mosquitoes, and the strong drink helped make you oblivious to them. The Patriots also proved surprisingly good both at cards and at conversation. But their bets were far lighter and their topics of conversation far heavier than Creighton was accustomed to.

The knights of the tavern were known to wager several pounds on a single hand; the Americans seldom put up more than a few pence, or the equivalent in *deniers* or *reales*. During one round of betting, Tom Paine casually pulled forth a hundred-dollar paper bill and tossed it onto the pile. The others laughed and hooted until, grinning, he withdrew it. Creighton leaned over to Peter. "What was that about?"

"Continental money. 'Twas put out by the United States government—while the government lasted. It's as useless as an old almanac now."

Creighton's friends back in Bristol had little use for politics or morals; the talk at the Café des Exiles, though it touched on many things, never strayed far from these two issues. Between hands of cards, a man named Burr was holding forth on what he called "the Indian situation."

Creighton gathered that there were two main groups of Indians in the area—the Chickasaws and the Choctaws. The Choctaws had traditionally been allies of the French, but Burr was concerned that the British were buying their loyalty with gifts of food, weapons, and other trade goods. "Already there have been Indian raids on Côte des Allemands and on some of the outlying plantations. How long, gentlemen, before they attack New Orleans?"

A large-nosed fellow whose name Creighton couldn't quite recall—Poultry, or Mouldy, or something of the sort—nodded gravely as he raked in his winnings. "Burr's fears are well founded. The Brits did the same thing in Carolina. The governor and his military aide decided they'd pass out muskets to the Cherokees." Creighton's attention turned abruptly from the card game to the conversation. The Carolina governor's military aide had been none other than Colonel Gower. "Then they proceeded to convince the Indians," Mouldy-Poultry went on, "that us Back Country Patriots were their enemies. They'd surely have wiped us out to a man, except we were warned that the redskins were coming, and were ready for them."

"Didn't I hear that it was a Brit who brought the word to you?" asked Paine.

"It was. Which goes to show, I guess, that they an't all bad." Mouldy-Poultry assembled the deck of cards and began shuffling it. "He was a major in the British army, as a matter of fact—though you'd never have guessed it, except for the uniform. He was a good-looking, good-natured fellow, soft-spoken and quick to laugh. I remember him well because he was the one decent Englishman I've met." Mouldy-Poultry glanced at Creighton. "Present company excepted, of course." The man scratched his prominent nose. "Come to think on it, bub, his name was the same as yours. Brown. Harry Brown." He dealt a hand to each of the players.

Peter laughed. "What about that? Any relation, Creighton?"

Creighton didn't reply. He automatically picked up his cards, but couldn't think what to do with them. He felt as though he'd been struck hard on the head again. Could there have been more than one Major Harry Brown stationed in Carolina?

Paine said, "Did the Brits ever find out it was this Brown fellow that warned you?"

"They did," said Mouldy-Poultry. "And I'm ashamed to say it was one of our boys that told them, in exchange for a few pounds and a pardon. They court-martialed the major, of course, and shipped him off to Florida to hang. They knew better than to do it in Charles Town, for we'd have done our best to save him."

Creighton threw down his cards. "I'm out," he managed to say, then strode from the room, his head throbbing, his eyes smarting with tears. Outside, he was assailed at once by mosquitoes, but he ignored them; they tormented him far less than his own thoughts. He had always believed that his father had died honorably, fighting bravely against the rebels. It was what Colonel Gower had told him and his mother.

But it seemed that the colonel had only been trying to spare his sister the shameful truth: Her husband had been hanged for aiding the enemy. That explained why, when Creighton had asked about his father's death back in Charles Town, Colonel Gower had put him off. And of course his uncle had another motive for withholding the truth. It had been his idea to arm the Cherokees and send them against the Back Country settlers. That meant he was also responsible, at least indirectly, for Harry Brown's fate.

By now, nothing Gower did, however despicable, would have surprised Creighton. But how could his father, who had always preached to Creighton the value of honor, do something so dishonorable as to help the enemy?

The night before Harry Brown departed for the Colonies, they had talked about duty and loyalty. As he sat watching the major polish his saber, Creighton had said, "Be sure to kill as many Yankeys as possible, will you?"

His father had given him an odd look, almost reproachful, and said, "I hope it won't come to that."

Creighton was taken aback by this. "You're not *afraid* to fight them, are you?"

Major Brown considered a moment. "No," he said finally. "I just hope we may find a way yet to settle our differences without shooting one another."

"Then why are you going?" Creighton demanded, distressed by his father's obvious lack of rancor toward the hated Yankeys. "Why don't you resign your commission?"

The major tested the keenness of the saber with his thumb and, satisfied with it, slid it into its sheath. "I've sworn loyalty to my country," he said. "If it goes to war, then I'm bound by duty to go with it." Creighton was sure his father had meant those words, and believed them. And yet, when his loyalty was put to the test, it had failed.

He heard heavy footsteps coming up behind him, and a moment later Peter said, "Creighton? Is something wrong?"

Creighton swiped at his tear-filled eyes and cleared his throat. "My . . . um . . . my head is hurting again."

"I an't much good at reading people, but you seemed upset back there." When Creighton didn't reply, the giant said hesitantly, "I was only joking about you being related to that British major. I vow, I didn't mean nothing by it. 'Twas a stupid thing to say."

"No," Creighton said faintly, almost inaudibly. "You were right. He was my father."

"Your father?" Peter walked beside him in silence for a minute or two before he settled on something more to say. "I'm sorry. It must have been hurtful, being reminded of— of all that."

"It wasn't a case of being reminded. I never knew. I thought he died in battle, not at the end of a rope."

"You sound as though you're ashamed. But you shouldn't be."

"*Why* shouldn't I be?" Creighton demanded. "He was a traitor!"

"A traitor? Because he wouldn't sit by and let the Indians massacre a parcel of innocent men and their families?"

"You can hardly call them innocent. They were rebels."

"In their sympathies, I warrant you. But they hadn't taken up arms, and they hadn't taken no English lives. They were hunters and farmers, not soldiers. 'Twas the governor who was at fault, not your father. Your father did what his conscience told him to. By my lights, that don't make him a traitor; it makes him a hero."

There was that word again: *conscience.* As far as Creighton was concerned, it was in the same league with mosquitoes—an infernal nuisance, one that could not be chased away for long, no matter how hard you tried.

As he had on so many other nights lately, Creighton lay awake for a long while, trying to sort out his thoughts and his feelings. He was no more used to it than he was to doing manual labor. Back in Bristol, the world had seemed simple and orderly. Every person, place, and thing could be neatly classified: A person was either upper-class or lower-class, English or not English; a place was either civilized or uncivilized; a thing was either good or bad, right or wrong.

But since he'd left England, the boundaries between those categories seemed to have grown indistinct. Or maybe they had just shifted position, the way the Mississippi River sometimes did. Theoretically, everything east of the river was English territory and everything west of it belonged to Spain. But Franklin said that each time the river flooded, it cut a new and slightly different path, so land that had been on one side of the river was now on the other.

Back home, Creighton had always been comfortably certain which side of any given line he was on. But the flood of events in which he'd been caught up had left him floundering, uncertain which shore to swim to. He longed for that old certainty, that world in which things were painted so clearly in black and white.

Perhaps that was why, in the weeks that followed, he threw himself so wholeheartedly into his duties in the printing shop. In that small world, everything seemed clearer: black print on white paper, seeking out words that were wrong and making them right.

He still made mistakes of his own from time to time. When he was allowed to ink the type for the first time, he absentmindedly laid the roller down on Sophie's stool. Luckily, she discovered it before she sat down. It was lucky, too, that this was her week to practice tolerance. Though she hadn't quite mastered humility yet, Franklin thought it best for her to move on to something less challenging, and return to humility later, when she had reached a higher level of enlightenment.

Chapter FIFTEEN

One task Franklin hadn't asked him to help with was the printing of *The Liberty Tree*. Apparently the old man had done the job himself, for one day the form of type that had been concealed under the cloth was gone. But if Franklin had meant for the paper to remain a secret, he was soon disappointed.

One day, as he and Creighton were mixing varnish, linseed oil, and lampblack to make a new batch of ink, Benedict Arnold stormed into the shop, brandishing a sheet of paper as though it were a sword. "I can't believe you would print this!" he shouted, and flung the paper down in front of Franklin.

"And I can't believe," the old man said calmly, "that you're so indiscreet as to show this to anyone and everyone." He picked up the paper, but not before Creighton had recognized it as a copy of *The Liberty Tree*.

Arnold glared at Franklin, then at Creighton. "What? The boy knows about this, doesn't he?"

"He didn't . . . until now."

Arnold seemed as angry at himself now as at Franklin. "I assumed he'd helped you print it."

"No. But I suppose there's no harm done. I think that we can trust him. Eh, Creighton?"

"Of course." Creighton didn't think it wise to reveal that he'd been aware of the paper's existence for some time.

"Now," Franklin said to Arnold, "what are you so outraged about?"

"You know well enough." Arnold flicked the paper derisively with one hand. "This essay—if it can be called that—written by Anonymous, otherwise known as Aaron Burr."

Franklin gave the essay a look of feigned puzzlement. "I thought it was quite well written."

"That's not the question, as you also know. The question is, why do we waste our time trying to convince the western territories to secede, when we should be calling on all Americans to rise up and drive the British out?"

"We tried that, if you recall, and failed. It's time we tried something else, something that may not involve going to war."

Arnold made a disparaging noise. "You really believe England is going to give up the western territories without a fight? If we're going to have to do battle with them again, it may as well be for the prize we really want, not just what we're willing to settle for."

"We're in no position to fight anyone for anything," Franklin said. "We have no army."

"We can raise one, given a little time. The capture of the *Amity* put several thousand pounds in our coffers and doubled the size of our armory."

"And if we should raise an army, who will lead it? You?"

Arnold lowered his gaze. "I'm well aware that I could never command the same sort of loyalty Washington did. But as far as we know, he's still alive."

"Yes. Now if we only knew where." Franklin put a hand on Arnold's arm. "I'd be as happy as anyone to have Washington back among us. Perhaps he could get us all pulling together again, rather than each of us straining in a different direction. And perhaps it will happen. But in the meantime, we must do the best we can to keep our cause alive. You're doing what you do best—capturing ships and money and munitions. Let me continue to do what I do best—winning minds and hearts."

Arnold didn't seem convinced, but at least he seemed calmer. "It's not the idea of creating a new country out of the western lands that I object to so much as the notion of getting France and Spain involved. Being ruled by a Louis or a Charles would be no better than being ruled by a George—a good deal worse, in fact, since they would try to turn us all into Catholics."

"No one is proposing that we become a part of Spain, only that we form an alliance against Britain." Franklin held the paper out to Arnold. "Here. Read it again, with a more open mind this time."

Arnold grudgingly took the sheet and left the shop. Franklin said, "There you see one reason why we lost the war."

"General Arnold?"

Franklin laughed. "Well, not him specifically. He's a good soldier, if a bit hotheaded. I meant the inability to agree on anything. Washington seemed able, somehow, to find a path everyone could agree upon—or at least he could make them think they agreed." The old man poured another cup of linseed oil into the ink. "You know, I once saw a snake that had two separate heads on a single body. Now, you would think, wouldn't you, that with two brains it would be twice as intelligent? Instead, it seemed unable to make up its mind—or its minds, should I say?—to go anywhere, or even to eat, so it simply lay there until it starved to death. We're more helpless, even, than that. We're like a snake with no head at all."

"In England," Creighton said, "we heard half a dozen conflicting rumors about Washington's fate. Some said that he'd turned his coat and joined our side, others that he'd deserted and gone to France, still others that he'd been blown to pieces by a cannonball."

Franklin shook his head. "None of those is true. He was taken during the British invasion of New York. I got a full account of his capture from one of his aides. It seems that when our boys saw how many troops they were up against, they turned tail. Now, Washington is normally a reasonable, restrained sort of man, but he does have a temper, and when it gets loose it's far more fearsome even than Arnold's. When his men began deserting him in droves, he exploded. He rode among them lashing out with his riding crop like a madman and bellowing like a bull, ordering them to stand and fight. When they paid him no heed, Washington flung his hat in the dirt and shouted to the heavens, 'Are these the men with which I am to defend America?' Then apparently he was exhausted by his own fury, for he slumped in his saddle in a sort of stupor, as though he had no notion of where he was, or what danger he was in. Several of his men turned back to help him, but the British got to him first."

"You think he's is in prison somewhere, then?"

"So our informants say. But no one seems to know where. We've put out a plea for information on the matter in this issue of *The Liberty Tree*."

Creighton didn't let on that this was old news to him. Though he'd done his bit of spying only under duress, he knew that it would seem to Franklin and Sophie as though he'd betrayed them. In fact, it had begun to seem that way to Creighton himself.

A week ago, he wouldn't have cared what they thought of him. But like a sailor who suddenly discovers that the wind, which had been blowing against him, has changed direction, Creighton realized that, without his even noticing, his feelings about them had turned around.

His feelings about his uncle had changed, too. He had never liked the man much, but what he felt now was something far stronger than mere dislike. If Gower had ever demonstrated anything resembling kindness or decency, the blow he'd delivered to Creighton's head had erased all memory of it. Though the lump had all but disappeared, the pain still plagued him from time to time. So did thoughts of his father. Each time they did, he silently cursed the colonel, and he would have prayed for the Indians or the alligators to get him except that it would mean sending Lieutenant Hale to the same fate.

He was no longer so eager to return to English territory, either. If it meant returning to his uncle, he would as soon stay in New Orleans, mosquitoes and all. But, as much as he might wish it, he had not seen or heard the last of Colonel Gower.

On Thursday afternoon, the new issue of the *New Orleans Weekly Journal* "hit the streets," as Dr. Franklin put it. Weary from his efforts, Creighton went to bed early that night, but he woke a few hours later, feeling vaguely uneasy.

It took him a moment to determine what had disturbed his sleep.

There was an acrid smell in the room, as though someone had been smoking a particularly foul cigar. Then he became aware of a crackling sound. He sat up and looked around, and saw flames outside his window. The wooden shingles on the roof of the printing shop were ablaze.

He flung aside the mosquito netting and stumbled to the window. In the light from the flames he saw three figures, dressed only in Indian-style breechcloths, sloshing buckets full of some liquid onto the log walls of the building. At first he thought it was water and assumed that they were attempting to douse the fire. Then he caught the scent of tar and noticed the torches in their hands.

"What are you doing?" he cried, and without stopping to think or even to don his breeches, he sprang out the window and across the yard. Two of the Indians took to their heels; the third lingered long enough to thrust his smoldering torch into the tar in an attempt to set it afire. When it failed, he threw down the torch and turned to run, but too late. Creighton launched himself at the man, grabbed him about the knees, and brought him crashing to the ground.

The Indian struggled fiercely for a moment and then, unable to free himself, squirmed onto his back and reached for something at his waist. Creighton had little experience in hand-to-hand fighting; it was considered beneath a gentleman's dignity. But desperation is an excellent teacher. He raised one arm and drove his elbow as hard as he could into his adversary's groin. The man gave an agonized cry and doubled over.

Creighton groped about until he found what the man had been reaching for—a hunting knife. He slipped the knife from its leather sheath and got to his knees. The whole roof of the printing shop was in flames now. He glanced about uncertainly. He couldn't let the building burn, but if he went for help, or even if he pumped water himself to throw on the flames, it would mean letting his prisoner escape.

Just then Sophie ran from the house, dressed in her nightgown. *"Mon Dieu!"* she gasped, staring first at the flames then at Creighton, who stood over a groaning, half-naked man, holding a knife in his hand and wearing nothing but his underclothing.

"Do you have a fire brigade here?" Creighton called over the crackle of the fire.

"Oui! I will ring the alarm!" She flew off down the street, barefoot, her nightgown billowing out behind her.

A moment later Franklin limped into the yard, took one look at the situation, and said, as calmly as though this sort of thing happened every day, "We must rescue the types. Come with me."

"What about this knave? We can't just let him go!"

"The types are more important." Franklin pushed open the door to the shop and disappeared inside.

Creighton hesitated. If he kicked the Indian hard enough, it might at least slow him down. But it wouldn't be a gentlemanly thing to do. He flung the knife as far as he could into the darkness and hurried after Dr. Franklin.

The roof had already burned through in several places, and the flames illuminated the room with a flickering, insubstantial light. Franklin had two of the type bins in his arms and was shuffling toward the door. "It's useless!" Creighton said. "We'll never be able to save them all!"

"Then we'll save what we can," Franklin replied, his voice strained, breathless.

Creighton sighed and hefted two of the bins. "What about the printing press?"

"It can be replaced," Franklin called over his shoulder. "The types cannot."

As he carried a second load of type into the yard, Creighton heard the alarm bell in the square clanging. But he knew that by the time the fire brigade arrived, it would be too late. Already the roof was on the verge of falling in. He glanced toward the spot where his adversary had been lying; the man was gone. Shaking his head in disgust, Creighton plunged into the building again and hauled out two more bins of type. As he stood with his hands propped on his knees, trying to get his breath, he saw Franklin start into the shop yet again. "No!" he called. "Let the rest go! It's not safe!"

Franklin ignored him. Cursing under his breath—what little he had—Creighton headed after the old man. Just as he reached the door, there was a creaking, snapping sound from above. The timbers in the center of the roof collapsed and crashed to the floor. "Doctor!" Creighton burst through the doorway. The composing table lay buried under flaming debris. Choking on the smoke, Creighton dropped to the floor and crawled forward on his hands and knees. "Doctor!"

The heat was so intense it felt as though it were blistering his skin, but he forced himself on, one arm shielding his face, until he caught sight of Franklin's still, crumpled form. The old man lay under the composing table, which had helped shelter him from the falling beams. Creighton crawled the last few yards on his belly. Reaching out, he took hold of the neck of Franklin's nightshirt and tugged. The old man wouldn't budge.

Creighton turned around, planted his feet against the legs of the table, and heaved. The body slid toward him a foot or two, far enough so Creighton could grab hold of one of the old man's arms. He scrabbled on his back across the floor, dragging Franklin after him a few inches at a time. Another section of the roof caved in off to his left, making him struggle even more desperately for the door.

His throat burned, his lungs demanded fresh air, but when he drew a breath, he took in only the searing, smoke-filled air of the room. He doubled up, coughing and retching. He was certain that the door couldn't be more than a few yards away, but he was equally certain that he couldn't possibly drag Franklin's limp form that far—or his own, for that matter.

Chapter SIXTEEN

When Creighton was a young boy, his father had taken him to the county fair on May Day. Exhausted from so many new sights and sounds, the boy had fallen asleep in his father's arms. When he awoke later, he found himself in his own bed. It had seemed inexplicable, almost magical, to him, that he could fall asleep in one place and wake up in another.

That same sort of magic was at work again. One moment he was sprawled on the floor of the printing shop, enveloped by smoke and heat, and the next moment there was damp grass beneath him, and cool, humid air all around him, a hand supporting his head, a cup of water at his lips. He drank greedily, trying to quench the burning in his throat, but it only set him coughing again, and he spewed the water out.

"*Doucement,*" said a voice. "Just a little, for now."

Creighton pried his eyelids open enough to see Sophie bending over him. "How—how did I—"

"*Non, non,* no talking. Just rest. Peter pulled you out."

"And Dr. Franklin . . . ?"

She hesitated a moment, then said, "Yes, Dr. Franklin, too." She held the cup to his mouth again, but he pushed it aside and sat up. Someone had cleaned most of the dirt and soot from him and covered him with a blanket.

A dozen or more men were swarming about the printing shop, dousing the dying flames with buckets of water from the pump. Though the log walls were badly scorched in places, they still stood. Nothing remained of the roof except smoking rubble.

"He wanted to save the types," Creighton said, his words punctuated by coughs. "We didn't get even half of them."

"*Eh bien.* You did your best."

"I let the wretches who did it get away, too."

"Not all of 'em," another voice said. Creighton looked up at the giant form looming over him. Peter crouched down to his level. "We caught one. He ran smack into us, in fact—or hobbled, I should say. Somebody had knocked him about a tittle. Was that you?"

Creighton nodded. "Any idea who he is, or why they did it?"

"Well, he's done up to look like an Indian, but he an't. He's a Brit, from Fort Bute. General Arnold's been questioning him. It looks like Colonel Gower and Lieutenant Hale didn't go downriver, after all. They went upriver to the fort and told what they seen here." Peter glanced at the blackened building. "I'm guessing one of the things they told was where *The Liberty Tree* was being printed."

"But how could the prisoners know that?" Sophie said. "Who would have told them?"

Peter spread his hands helplessly. "I can't say. General Arnold thinks it could have been somebody from the

Amity's crew. But they didn't have any way of knowing, either." Creighton put his head in his hands. "Are you all right, Cray?" Peter asked anxiously.

"Just . . . just a little dizzy," Creighton murmured. But in truth, the effects of his ordeal seemed almost minor compared with the pangs of his conscience. How could he blame the British soldiers for setting the fire to the building when it was his information that led them to it? Of course they still would have known nothing if it hadn't been for Colonel Gower. He now had one more reason to hate the man.

"Well, we better put you to bed," Peter said. Before Creighton could protest, he was scooped up effortlessly in the giant's arms.

"I can walk," Creighton muttered, embarrassed.

"Poh, you an't heavy," Peter said cheerfully. "I could lift three of you."

As Creighton was carried through the door, he caught a glimpse of Sophie holding one hand over her mouth, concealing a laugh. A portly man in a powdered wig was just emerging from Franklin's chambers, carrying a black leather bag. Peter stopped and lowered his passenger. "How is he, Doctor?"

"Pas bien," the physician said. "His ribs are crushed, and his limbs are badly burned."

"Can we see him?" Creighton asked.

The man shook his head. "He would not know you. I have given him an opiate to ease the pain."

As Peter helped him to his room and into bed, Creighton said, "I tried to tell him not to go in. I said it wasn't safe. He wouldn't listen."

"Well, he put a parcel of effort and money into bringing those types here from Philadelphia. I guess he didn't want to lose them."

"Still, it wasn't worth risking his life for, was it?"

Peter sat carefully on the chair. "I guess it was, to him. Anyway, you risked your life, too."

"For him, not for the types." Creighton was racked by another bout of coughing, and had to sit up in order to breathe. When it had passed, he said, "Why did he come here, anyway? Why didn't he stay in Philadelphia?"

Peter stared at him incredulously. "He really would have been risking his life if he did that."

"He was only a diplomat, not a soldier. They wouldn't have harmed him, would they?"

The giant gave a humorless laugh. "You have a better opinion of the Brits than I do, I warrant."

Creighton lay back on his pillows and considered all the things his countrymen had done that he wouldn't have thought them capable of: beating a man bloody for reading a subversive newspaper; plotting to massacre hundreds of unsuspecting settlers; leaving the families of the rebels destitute. "No," he said at last. "Not really. Not any longer."

Peter got to his feet. "I'll leave you to rest now."

Creighton nodded. "I never thanked you for pulling me out of there."

The giant shifted about uncomfortably. "It wasn't nothing."

"You consider two lives nothing?" Creighton asked, with mock indignation.

"I didn't mean it that way."

"I know. Anyway, thank you."

"You're welcome."

As Peter turned to go, the door to Creighton's room opened and Arnold stuck his head in. "There you are, Peter. Come—we're holding a meeting at the Café to discuss how we'll retaliate against the English." He glanced at Creighton. "You can join us, if you want."

Creighton hesitated, uncertain how to respond, uncertain where his loyalties lay. Peter answered for him. "He's too weak. He'd do better to rest."

Arnold nodded. "That was a brave thing you did," he said gruffly. "We're grateful to you. Your father would be proud."

Creighton was seized by another coughing fit. When he got his breath back, he said, "You—you knew my father?"

"No. But I know what he did."

"I told him what you told me," Peter said. "I hope you don't mind."

Creighton dropped his gaze, still unsure how he felt about his father's actions.

"You know," Arnold said, "men who have never been on a battlefield imagine that it requires a good deal of courage." He rubbed absently at his injured leg, as though recalling how it felt to be in battle. "But the truth is, courage requires thought, and there's not much thought involved in fighting a battle. It's mostly a matter of duty, of dumbly obeying orders. It's a far more difficult thing to make up your own mind about what's right and act accordingly—to go against the demands of duty when it's necessary, to take another path when you feel the one you've been led down is wrong. That requires real courage."

Arnold and Peter departed before Creighton could put into words the question that was foremost in his mind: With no one to guide you, how can you know which path is the right one?

When Creighton woke in the morning, his chest ached and his throat felt raw, but he was more concerned about Franklin's welfare than about his own. As soon as he dressed, he headed for the old man's room. Sophie was already there, changing the dressings on Franklin's left leg and arm, which had been scorched by the burning roof beams.

The opiate had apparently begun to wear off, for Franklin was tossing about, muttering words that were, by turns, inaudible and unintelligible. Creighton didn't need to ask about the old man's condition; he could read the answer in Sophie's face. "Could you bring a glass of brandy, *s'il vous plaît?* The *médecin* left some opiate, to be given to him when the pain returned."

Creighton brought the brandy and watched as Sophie stirred a spoonful of brown powder into the glass. "Hold his head," she instructed, and spooned the mixture into the old man's mouth. After a time, Franklin's tossing and muttering ceased and he lay still. But for the irregular sound of his breathing, he might have been taken for dead.

Throughout the morning, Franklin's fellow Patriots came by, singly and in groups, sat for a time, then departed again, saddened and silent, leaving Creighton and Sophie to watch over the old man and wait. They pretended they were waiting for him to recover, but it was a feeble pretense, and Creighton held as little hope of it as he did of the ruined printing shop rising from its ashes.

Creighton had seen men die before, but always life had been extinguished quickly, by the jerk of a rope or, in Captain Pierce's case, by the flight of a cannonball; the boundary between life and death had been stark and clear. There was no clear end to Franklin's life; it seemed instead to drain away imperceptibly, as the water in the bowl atop his evaporative cooler disappeared, little by little, until suddenly the vessel was empty.

The Patriots had a brick mausoleum constructed to house the old man's body. In New Orleans, a standard burial was only for those who could not afford a tomb. The water level was so near the surface of the ground that holes had to be bored in the coffins so they wouldn't float.

Creighton had grown up believing that a gentleman never made a display of his emotions—at least those emotions that might be construed as weakness. He was taken aback, then, to see several of the Americans weeping openly at Franklin's funeral.

Though Creighton hid his feelings, from old habit, it didn't mean that he felt nothing. On the contrary, if such a thing could have been measured, he was certain that the emotional burden he carried would have outweighed any other's. Not only did he feel a wrenching sadness over the passing of the old man, who had treated him more fairly and kindly than anyone had since his father's death, he was also tormented by guilt over the part he had played in Franklin's death. But even stronger than the sorrow or the remorse was his anger—at his uncle in particular, and at his countrymen in general.

In view of all that had happened these past few months, the British no longer seemed to him such a superior, civilized people. In fact, they had come to resemble, in his mind, all the tyrannical schoolmasters and bullying students he had ever known. And what had once been his homeland now seemed to him much the way Carolina and Florida and Louisiana had once seemed: an unfamiliar and inhospitable place, a country to which he no longer owed any loyalty.

Of the many virtues that Creighton had been taught were essential to a gentleman, loyalty seemed to rank above all others—loyalty to one's family name, to one's class, to one's country. That was why the news of his father's defection had stunned him so; Harry Brown seemed to have betrayed the most basic tenet of honor. But now Creighton understood for the first time the truth of the matter: If loyalty really was the most worthy of virtues, then loyalty that was misplaced or misguided must be the most worthless.

To his surprise, Sophie—who wasn't exactly known for hiding her emotions—remained dry-eyed throughout Franklin's funeral service. As Creighton and Peter walked her home, she explained why. "Dr. Franklin once told me that we should not grieve when another person dies, any more than we grieve when they go to sleep. He said . . . he said, 'I consider death to be as necessary to our constitution as sleep, and I am confident that I shall rise refreshed in the morning.' So, I—" Her voice broke. She wiped at her eyes and forced a smile. "I have determined not to weep for him."

"Have you thought about what you'll do now?" Peter asked.

Sophie seemed puzzled by the question. "Do?"

"Where you'll live, I mean. How you'll get by."

She shrugged. "I will go on living where I live now, and I will go on doing what I do now—printing the *Journal* each week."

"By *yourself?*"

"If it is necessary. But . . ." She gave him a glance that carried an unmistakable challenge. "I hoped that I might have *un peu d'assistance.*"

Peter looked distinctly uncomfortable. "Me? I don't know nothing about printing."

Creighton, who had been gloomily silent until now, spoke up suddenly. "I'll help." Peter looked at him in surprise. "Well," Creighton said, "she's right, you know; it is what Dr. Franklin would have wanted."

"I suppose." Peter shook his head. "But the printing shop . . . It's a shambles. How will you . . . ?"

"I am accustomed to hard work," Sophie said. "Besides, there again I hope to have plenty of *assistance.*"

<hr />

Chapter SEVENTEEN

*A*ccording to Sophie, another of Dr. Franklin's favorite sayings was "It is useless to delay the inevitable." Apparently Sophie felt that this maxim also applied to the impossible, for they set about salvaging what they could of the printing shop that very afternoon.

The long leather aprons they wore when they were printing the paper had escaped unscathed; the day before the fire, Sophie had brought them into the house to be cleaned. Though Peter was given the longest apron, it reached barely to his knees, rather than a foot below them, as Sophie's and Creighton's did.

Even with the aprons to protect them, their skin and clothing quickly became caked with soot and ashes. To keep from choking on the stuff, they tied cloths around their mouths and noses. A month earlier, or even a week, Creighton would never have imagined he was capable of doing such backbreaking labor, let alone enjoying it. Well, perhaps *enjoying* wasn't the right word; there was nothing remotely pleasant about it. He had thought he was working hard when he was slinging type forms about and working the printing press. But those jobs seemed like parlor games compared with the brutal, filthy work of cleaning up the burned building.

At the same time, though, it was satisfying, in a perverse sort of way. He had taken on the task of shoveling the smaller debris into a wooden barrow, which Sophie then wheeled off to the rear of the property and emptied. It somehow felt to Creighton as though he were scraping aside the mangled, useless remnants of his old life, and laying the foundations for a new one.

Peter's job was one that no one else could have dreamed of doing—moving aside the fallen roof timbers. Though some of the beams were almost whole, and were a good twenty feet in length, he pried them free of the rubble like so many jackstraws and, balancing one on each shoulder, carried them into the yard, where he stacked them in neat piles.

After a few hours of doing battle with the charred remains of the roof, Sophie called a temporary truce and went inside to fetch refreshments. Creighton collapsed onto a stool that had somehow survived intact. "Perhaps we should have asked some others to help."

Peter sat on a fallen beam and wiped the perspiration from his brow with his facecloth. "They're holding another war council—for all the good it'll do."

"What do you mean?"

"They won't agree on anything. They never do. Governor Galvez has already made his mind up to attack the British at Mobile. But the Patriots won't go along with that; at least most of 'em won't. They say it's too risky, that we should wait till we have more men and more ships."

"I'll wager that General Arnold doesn't share that opinion."

Peter laughed. "You'd win that wager. He'd want to attack the Brits if he had only half a dozen men, or even just one or two." He shook his head. "Sometimes I think it wouldn't matter much who he was attacking, either. He'd fight the French or the Spanish, I warrant, given half a reason. He'd sooner take any sort of action than just sit around drinking and discussing what to do, and not doing nothing. He says he feels like a ship with the wind in its sails and its anchor in the mud."

"And you?" Creighton said. "What do you think?"

The giant shrugged. "Nobody cares what I think. That's why I'm here, and not at the meeting."

"I care, or I wouldn't have asked."

He scratched his cheek thoughtfully, leaving behind long streaks of soot. "I believe that we ought to strike back at the Brits. But I don't believe we're ever going to, not without somebody leading us."

A sudden clattering sound made them turn toward the house. Sophie stood a few feet from them, hands on hips, next to a tray of tea things that she had obviously just set down, rather forcefully, on the upturned barrow. "I know that I am supposed to be practicing *tolerance* this week," she said. "But I will not tolerate talk of war, not here in Dr. Franklin's home. It is *irrespectueux* . . . disrespectful. You know that it was his wish to settle matters peacefully, not by fighting."

"I'm sorry," Peter murmured. He seemed content to leave it at that. Creighton was not.

"Dr. Franklin was an intelligent man," he said, "but in this case he was either very unobservant or very naive. I know the English, remember, and General Arnold is right—they never give up anything without a fight."

"That may be. But Americans say they do not wish to be part of England. So why do they insist on behaving just as the English do? Why can they not use *raison* . . . reason, instead of violence?"

"Because," Creighton said, "there are times when no amount of reason does any good. Have you ever heard it said that you must fight fire with fire?"

"That is a stupid saying." Sophie surveyed the burned building. "What would have happened, do you suppose, if we had thrown buckets of burning pitch on this fire, instead of buckets of water?"

"What would have happened," Creighton responded, "if your father and his countrymen had resisted the British, instead of letting themselves be driven from their land?"

Sophie glared at him a moment, arms crossed, then gave a quick sideways movement of her head. "*Allez-vous-en.*

Go. Both of you. I do not need your help. Go fight some-one." When Peter and Creighton hesitated, glancing uncer-tainly at one another, she stamped her foot. "*Je suis sérieuse!* I mean it! Go!"

"All right." Creighton took off his apron, tossed it aside, and stalked off.

After a moment Peter caught up with him. "You made her angry," the giant said reproachfully.

"*She* made *me* angry," Creighton snapped. "I was taught that if someone does you an injury, you don't just turn the other cheek; you strike back. It's a matter of honor."

"That's the same thing General Arnold always says."

"You don't agree?"

Peter scratched his chin again, smearing the streaks of soot. "I don't know, exactly. I admire him. But I admire Dr. Franklin, too."

"Yes, well, he's dead. And those responsible for it should be made to pay dearly." Though he was speaking of Franklin, he might as well have been talking about the death of Major Harry Brown.

"There he is now," Peter said.

Creighton looked up, startled, half expecting to see his father strolling toward them in that easygoing manner that was so unlike a military man—hands thrust into his pock-ets, hat tilted back on his head, whistling some tune whose words he could never manage to recall.

But the figure approaching them was nothing like his fa-ther. This man strode along with a sort of fierce determination, his arms not swinging freely but held at his sides as though poised to draw a weapon.

Peter touched the brim of his hat in a sort of salute. "Good afternoon, sir."

Unexpectedly, Arnold grinned—though this, too, had a fierce quality about it. "It *is* a good afternoon, Peter, and an unusual one. The Sons of Liberty have finally agreed on a course of action." He took Peter's arm. "Come; we'll have a drink, and I'll tell you all about it." Turning back, he nodded to Creighton. "You, too. I think this will interest you."

When they were seated in the nearest tavern with pints of ale before them, Arnold explained. The Patriots, he said, had decided to cooperate with the Spanish in an attack on the British. But there was a condition attached: In return, the Spanish would send an expedition into British territory to free General Washington.

"Gad," said Peter. "How can they do that when nobody knows where he is?"

Arnold gave that fierce grin again. "That's what we're being sent to find out."

"We?" Peter said. "You mean, you and me?"

Arnold glanced in Creighton's direction. "And Mr. Brown, here."

Creighton blinked in surprise. "Me?"

Arnold nodded. "If you're game."

"*Game?* That must be a Yankey expression."

Arnold's dark eyebrows lowered in a scowl. "Don't turn English on me. I thought your sympathies were with us."

"I'm sorry. It was a bit of a jest. So, what role am I expected to play in all this?"

"The role of the loyal English subject who has escaped from the clutches of the evil Yankeys and returned gratefully to his own people. Peter and I will be the traitors who aided you in your escape."

"You think the British will believe you?"

Arnold shrugged. "Probably not. But they'll believe *you*. And to encourage their belief, we will divulge certain information of vital interest to them."

"What sort of information?"

"The size of our army; the number of ships we have; the amount of arms; when and where we plan to attack them—that sort of information . . . all totally false, of course. *Anti*-information, you might call it, or *counter*-information."

"To whom will we divulge this counterinformation?"

Arnold leaned back in his chair and took a draught of his ale, gazing at Creighton over the rim of the ale pot. "If you can't work that one out for yourself," he said, licking the foam from his thin lips, "you're not nearly as smart as I gave you credit for."

Creighton felt a sudden, painful twinge from the nearly healed wound on his head, and he winced involuntarily. "Colonel Gower," he said.

Chapter EIGHTEEN

*L*ike Mobile, Pensacola lay on the coast of West Florida. Since it was less than two hundred miles from New Orleans, they could reasonably assume that Lieutenant Hale and Colonel Gower had made their way there by now. Creighton knew it would take more than Indians or alligators, or even quicksand, to keep the colonel from carrying out his duty.

Not caring to attract the attention of British ships, Arnold chose for the voyage a sloop that was weathered enough to pass for a fishing vessel and small enough to be manned easily by the three of them. To Creighton's dismay, they also donned coarse trousers and tunics like those worn by fishermen. In fact, they *had* been worn by fishermen—and recently, judging from the smell. They couldn't borrow clothing large enough for Peter; an outfit had to be sewn especially for him. He trampled the items in the dirt to make sure they were appropriately crumpled and soiled.

Creighton had to take no such measures. Every inch of his clothing was liberally stained with substances he preferred not to identify, and they reeked of fish. Still, he was willing to endure almost anything if it meant a chance to settle the score with his uncle.

He knew that what they were undertaking was dangerous. The colonel was no fool. Though they had thought their story out carefully and rehearsed it over and over, Gower was sure to have some doubts about it. Arnold felt that the counterinformation they had prepared would put his doubts to rest. He also seemed certain that the colonel would welcome his former servant back with open arms. What he didn't know, of course, was that Creighton hadn't been a servant, and that the colonel had deliberately, heartlessly, left him behind.

Creighton wasn't so confident about their chances. One thing might work in his favor: the fact that his uncle considered him useless and incompetent. He might never suspect that Creighton was capable of making up his own mind about anything, of deciding for himself where his loyalties lay.

Growing up, Creighton hadn't had much chance to learn any practical skills. But he did know how to sail a boat. As soon as his son could walk, Harry Brown had, over his wife's objections, regularly taken him out in the Bristol Channel aboard the *Clyde*, a little sloop owned by Creighton's grandfather, Sir Robert. When the major went off to fight in America, Creighton had lost all interest in sailing, as he had in most of the other things his father had taught him.

Even though Arnold's boat was considerably larger than the *Clyde*, Creighton handled the rigging and the tiller with a deftness and confidence that seemed to surprise both Arnold and Peter. "I an't much of a sailor, myself," Peter confessed. He regarded his huge hands accusingly. "Too clumsy, I guess. Give me something to lift or to pound, and I'm all right, but tying and untying knots . . ." He sighed. "And navigation? I tried to learn to use a sextant once." He shook his head mournfully. " 'Twas was never the same after that."

Creighton laughed sympathetically. With a furtive glance toward Arnold, who sat forward of the mast, Peter leaned in toward Creighton and said softly, "You know, I an't any good at deceiving folk, neither. I've tried, and they always seem to see through me. I'm afraid that no matter how many times we go over what we're to say, I'm going to give us away, somehow."

"Have you told him this?" Creighton asked, inclining his head toward the bow.

"Gad, no!" Peter said, as though the very prospect upset him. "I don't want him thinking I'm a coward. I an't. I just don't want to go botching up the plan, the way I did the sextant."

Perhaps, Creighton thought, the giant was right; perhaps he was just too honest at heart to lie convincingly. "Do you want me to tell him?" he suggested.

Peter brightened. "Would you? You could explain it better."

"I'll try."

"Thank you." Peter seized his free hand and shook it gratefully—and painfully. "You're a good friend."

Creighton didn't reply. He was thinking of how he'd obtained the pistol so underhandedly, at Peter's expense.

When he privately broached the subject to Arnold, Creighton made it seem as though leaving Peter out of the plan were his idea. "The fewer players we have in the game," he said, "the less chance that someone will accidentally show his hand."

Arnold stared at him a moment, as though offended by the proposal. Then, to Creighton's surprise, he said, "Your point is well taken." Arnold drummed his fingers thoughtfully on the gunwales. "However, I don't want Peter thinking that I don't trust him. I do. I'd trust him with my life."

"I understand," Creighton said. "Don't worry; I'll tell him it was my idea."

To enter Pensacola Harbor, they had to sail through a narrow strait between two long, narrow islands—a passage guarded by a British fort. Though Arnold doubted that the garrison there would fire upon an innocent-seeming fishing vessel, he preferred to wait until dark to slip past the fort. They wouldn't be able to make out any channel markers, but with the sloop's shallow draft, it was unlikely they'd run aground.

Once night fell, they passed the fort unnoticed and unchallenged and dropped anchor a hundred yards or so from the city's quay, amid a small fleet of bona fide fishing boats. They slept aboard the sloop and, in the morning, rowed ashore in the dinghy. As Peter shipped the oars and prepared to disembark, Arnold took hold of his sleeve. "Wait."

The general drew a knife from a sheath at his waist and, lifting the hem of his tunic, began picking at the stitches with the point of the weapon. "I've a task for you—one that's as important as ours." From the fold of the hem he withdrew a sheet of paper that had been rolled tightly. "I want you to find the Boar's Head Tavern and deliver this to the proprietor, a fellow with the curious name of Pedro O'Reilly. He's a Patriot sympathizer." Arnold handed the paper to Peter. "As I'm sure you realize, you dare not let this fall into anyone else's hands. What it contains is not counterinformation, but the real thing."

Peter nodded solemnly. After looking about his person for several moments, obviously wondering where best to hide the paper, he thrust it into his shoe. "Where should we meet, and when?"

"At the tavern. If we don't turn up in two days' time, it will mean . . . well, if we don't turn up, I want you and O'Reilly to take the sloop and return to New Orleans. Will you do that?"

The giant stared at him, as though not certain Arnold was serious. "Leave you here, you mean? I—I couldn't—"

"Those are your orders, Corporal. Can I trust you to carry them out?"

Peter swallowed hard and nodded again. "Yes, sir."

"Good." Arnold shook his hand. "We'll see you in a day or two, then, with any luck."

As Peter climbed onto the wharf and strode off, Creighton said, "I thought you were confident that our plan would succeed."

"I am," Arnold replied. "But as Dr. Franklin was fond of saying, 'Expect the best; prepare for the worst.' "

———

The harbor was guarded by a massive stockade fort. Across the city square from the fort lay the State House. As they neared it, Creighton felt the pain in his skull returning; he stopped and put a hand to his head.

Arnold regarded him with an expression that seemed more contemptuous than concerned. "Are you sure you're up to this?"

"Yes, yes. Just give me a moment." Creighton drew a deep breath and tried to convince himself that this was just another role he was playing, no different from those he had played in school theatricals. But there was a difference: Back then, if he turned in an unconvincing performance, the worst he could expect was a few catcalls from the audience. If he failed in this performance, he was likely to suffer the same fate as his father.

His mother had said often enough that he would leave this world at the end of a rope. But she had assumed it would be his wild behavior that did him in. She would never have imagined—nor would he—that he might put his neck in jeopardy by turning traitor. Well, if he was bound to prove her prediction true, better it should happen in the service of a cause than as punishment for some petty crime.

"All right," he said at last. "I'm ready."

Before they reached the State House, a stocky, uniformed figure emerged from it. For a moment Creighton failed to recognize him, his uniform was so uncharacteristically neat and spotless. "Lieutenant Hale!" He hurried forward, forcing himself to smile broadly.

Hale seemed not to recognize him at first, either, probably because of the grimy tunic he wore. Then the lieutenant's face broke into a grin. "Good Lord! Creighton!" He shook the boy's hand enthusiastically. "How did you manage to escape, lad?"

"I had General Arnold's help." He gestured toward the general, who lagged several yards behind.

Hale glanced toward the American with a look that held equal amounts of astonishment and suspicion. *"Arnold?"*

Creighton nodded. "He's come over to y—to *our* side."

Hale frowned doubtfully. "Why?"

"He's lost faith in the Patriots, he says."

"And you believe him?" Hale kept his voice low so Arnold couldn't hear.

"Why shouldn't I? Why else would he help me?"

"I don't know. To gain our trust, maybe, so he can spy on us."

"No, it's quite the opposite. He's prepared to tell you all about the Americans' plans."

"Is he?" Hale regarded the general thoughtfully. "Well, we'll see what Colonel Gower thinks." He approached Arnold and greeted him warily. "Sir. I must say, I'm surprised to see *you* here."

"You wouldn't be," Arnold replied, his voice convincingly bitter, "if you'd seen, as I have, the pitiful state into which the Patriot cause has fallen. They no longer talk of independence, only of revenging themselves upon the British— even if it means joining forces with Spain or France." He spat in the dirt, as though the words had left a foul taste in his mouth. "If I'm to serve a monarch, I'd rather it was one who speaks English and doesn't worship the pope."

Hale nodded. "I see. I'm sure the colonel—pardon me, the *lieutenant governor*—will want to hear what you have to say." He turned to Creighton. "I imagine you'd just as soon not talk to the colonel?"

"No, no, I don't mind seeing him," Creighton said with far more enthusiasm than he felt.

"Oh? I thought that after—"

Creighton interrupted Hale before he could reveal how and why the colonel had left him behind. "I've concluded that being with the colonel somewhere civilized is better than being on my own at the end of nowhere."

Hale laughed. "I don't know how civilized you'll find it here. It's still a far cry from England. And we have just as many mosquitoes as New Orleans—maybe even more."

"You must like it here well enough, to have stayed."

The lieutenant shrugged. "The colonel asked me to be his aide. It's something to do, until I'm given another ship-board command. My main objection to it is that he expects me to always look 'presentable' "—he flicked the front of his waistcoat with his fingertips, as though chasing invisible motes of dust—which he takes to mean 'perfect.' " He gave an amused glance at the fragrant fisherman's garments Creighton wore. "I seem to recall a time when you took *me* to task for my slovenly appearance."

It was a pity, Creighton thought later, that his uncle had no interest in card games. The man would never have to worry about betraying his hand, for he was a master at guarding his emotions. He gave no indication whether he was happy to see his nephew, or dismayed, relieved, or resentful. He only looked down his long nose at Creighton in that wolflike manner of his, and said, "You've saved me the trouble of sending a rescue party out after you." Though Creighton was certain the colonel would have done no such thing, he held his tongue.

Gower didn't appear particularly surprised by Arnold's defection, either, or particularly suspicious. He seemed to consider it perfectly logical, as though anyone in his right mind would, of course, side with the British. If the colonel bore any grudge over the way the Americans had treated him, he showed no sign of it.

"We can use a man with your experience in battle," he told Arnold. "I'm sure there'll be a commission for you—not as a general, of course, but perhaps a major. I understand you have no love for the Spanish or the French."

"Quite the contrary," Arnold replied.

"Good. My government anticipates that hostilities with one or the other are inevitable. Perhaps you can help enlighten us on that matter."

"Yes. I expect I can."

Gower turned to Lieutenant Hale. "Will you see that my nephew is provided with suitable quarters?"

Arnold stared at him, then at Creighton. "Your nephew?"

The colonel gave him a curious look. "I assumed you knew that."

Arnold frowned and shook his head as though impatient with himself. "Of course. I was so used to thinking of him as your bound boy."

The colonel seemed to accept this. "If you will excuse us, gentlemen, Mr. Arnold and I have many things to discuss. Come; we'll have tea in my chambers . . . or do you prefer coffee?" The colonel made the question sound more like a challenge, or perhaps a test to determine just how loyal to England the general was prepared to be.

Arnold obviously recognized this, for he replied, "Tea will be very satisfactory, thank you."

Hale led Creighton across the street to the guardhouse, where he installed the boy in a room next to his own. "It's not spacious," the lieutenant admitted, "but I think you'll find it comfortable enough. The tick is filled with feathers and not dried grass like those in the barracks."

Creighton sat on the mattress and bounced lightly up and down. "It's fine. Better than I had back in New Orleans." He hoped his words sounded more sincere to Hale's ears than they did to his own. The truth was, for all its shortcomings, he would have much preferred to be back in New Orleans.

Though he hadn't dared admit it, even to himself, he had secretly been a little afraid that once he was back on English soil, his newfound loyalty to the American cause might fade. He needn't have worried. He felt like a stranger here, like an enemy, in fact, even to his uncle. Especially to his uncle.

The colonel might be able to put his old injuries and enmities aside, but Creighton couldn't. The wounds were too deep and too many. That Gower had caused Harry Brown to turn traitor and to hang would have been bad enough; he had compounded it by sealing Franklin's fate as well. Like the bruise left by Gower's pistol, the memory of these things nagged at Creighton constantly. Sometimes it was barely perceptible; other times it surged up with an intensity that nearly staggered him.

"Your head's still hurting you, I see," Hale said.

"What? Oh, only a little now and again."

"That was a nasty blow he dealt you—and an unnecessary one."

"Well, I shouldn't have insisted on going with you. It would have made your escape harder if I had."

"Maybe. It wasn't all that hard, though—aside from having to pole that plaguey boat upstream." Hale frowned at the memory, and laid a hand on the arm Creighton had accidentally winged.

"I'm truly sorry about shooting you. I hope it's healed all right."

"Oh, yes. I drenched it with brandy. It takes more than that to slow me down. Well, I'll let you settle in. If you need anything, let me know, will you?"

"Well, there is one thing I could use."

"What's that?"

Creighton plucked distastefully at the front of the smelly tunic. "Some new clothing."

Hale grinned. "Done." He started for the door, then turned back. "You never told Arnold you were the colonel's nephew, did you?"

Creighton hesitated, then shook his head.

"Why not?"

Despite the pain in his skull, Creighton managed to come up with a credible answer. "Because I wanted to be sure of his motives. I didn't want him helping me only in hopes of getting a reward from my uncle."

Hale laughed. "That's little chance of that. The colonel is as chary with his money as he is with his affections."

Creighton nodded glumly, thinking suddenly of his mother. As far as affections were concerned, at least, it was a family trait.

Chapter NINETEEN

C reighton awoke the next morning with the feeling that something was wrong. He lifted his head abruptly, and was immediately sorry that he had. The pain in his skull, which had subsided once he was left alone with no pressure upon him, had inexplicably returned.

Back in Bristol, he had felt this way nearly every morning—the aftereffects of a night of drinking and carousing. But he had gotten out of the habit lately. He actually found himself wishing for some of Sophie's bilious green tea with willow bark. And, now that he was thinking of Sophie, he wished that they had parted on better terms. When he returned—*if* he returned—he would have another apology to make. He groaned softly and, swinging his legs off the edge of the bed, sat up gingerly.

"You're a sorry sight," said a voice, startling Creighton so that his heart seemed to falter. He rubbed his gritty eyes and glanced about the room. His uncle sat in a chair by the window, fanning himself idly with a sheet of paper.

"What are you . . . ? Why are you . . . ?" Creighton murmured incoherently.

"We need to talk." It was clear from his tone that it wasn't family memories he meant to discuss.

"Now? Can't it wait until I've dressed, at least?"

"No. It's waited too long as it is." Gower turned from the window and faced Creighton. "Your fellow conspirator has given you away."

"What?" Creighton scowled, unable to make sense of his uncle's words. "What do you mean, given me away?"

"He's admitted to me the real reason you're here."

Creighton's heart sank. His uncle must be referring either to Arnold or Peter. In any case, it meant the game was up. But Creighton had learned that a game is never really lost until you show your hand, and he had no intention of showing his, not this early in the game. Instead, he bluffed, putting on a mask of innocent befuddlement. "What reason is that?"

"To obtain information for your American friends."

"Friends?" Creighton laughed. "The Americans? I don't even consider Arnold my friend."

"Apparently he's not, since he's betrayed you."

Creighton shrugged nonchalantly. "It could only be called a betrayal if it were the truth."

"Why would he lie?"

"I can't imagine," Creighton said, and his bafflement was genuine. Why *would* Arnold choose to betray him so suddenly and unexpectedly? Had the colonel somehow forced the truth from him? Tortured him, perhaps? He wouldn't doubt that Gower was capable of it. Or had Arnold confessed voluntarily, for some reasons of his own? But *what* reasons?

The only one Creighton could come up with—and admittedly he wasn't thinking too clearly just now—was that Arnold really had gone over to the British, and was sacrificing Creighton to them as proof of his loyalty. Or could he have remained true to the American cause, and given Creighton up only so he would *seem* to be aiding the British?

Creighton's mind, already muddled with sleep and with pain, couldn't hope to find the logic in all this, if there was any. All he could do was to go on bluffing, proclaiming his innocence, and let the colonel try to prove him guilty.

"He's done far more than just sell you out." The colonel pointed his paper at Creighton, and Creighton glanced at the sheet briefly, wondering whether it contained something that might further incriminate him. "He's also betrayed his fellow rebels by giving me detailed information about their plans."

That much, at least, was no surprise. Feeding the British false information was all part of the ruse they had worked out. "Of course," Creighton said. "He has no sympathy for the Patriots any longer."

The colonel leaned forward and fixed his lead-gray eyes on Creighton's face, as though searching for some telltale sign of deception. "Are you certain of that?"

Creighton kept his mask firmly in place. "As certain as I am that *I* have no sympathy for them."

Gower sat back in his chair. To Creighton's surprise, a slight, sardonic smile formed at the corners of his thin mouth. "Good." He began fanning himself with the paper again.

Good? Creighton thought. He was even more baffled by this new tack his uncle was taking. Still he said nothing, only waited.

"I must confess," the colonel said, "that I had serious doubts about you, and about Mr. Arnold. But now I believe that you're telling me the truth."

"You actually thought I'd gone over to the Americans?" Creighton said, making his voice sound hurt and reproachful.

"I thought it possible," Gower said. Creighton expected him to add, *After all, your father did it.* He didn't say that, but Creighton was sure he was thinking it. "The only way I could be sure was to confront you, to behave as though I *knew* you were guilty, and see how you reacted."

Creighton was glad he'd been so cautious. "Arnold didn't really accuse me of anything, then?"

The colonel shook his head. "That was merely a strata-gem of mine, calculated to make you reveal your true colors—and his. I knew that if he had in fact been a spy, you would have betrayed him, just as you thought he had betrayed you."

Creighton made his sigh of relief sound like one of bewilderment. "This is all too confusing for me, particularly considering I'm only half-awake."

"That was part of the stratagem—catching you in an unguarded moment, when you were more likely to let the truth slip out."

"Well, now that I've passed your test, do you mind if I go back to sleep?"

"Not yet," the colonel said. "I've one more thing to discuss." He held out the paper with which he'd been fanning himself. "I couldn't show this to you until I was certain I could trust you."

Puzzled, Creighton took the sheet and unfolded it. For the first time, he noticed how crumpled and creased it was, as though it had been rolled up tightly and flattened, then smoothed out again. It contained five lines of numbers, arranged in clumps of three or four. Creighton swallowed hard several times, until he could make his voice sound normal. "What is this?"

"A coded message, obviously. I should think you'd recognize it."

He did recognize it, of course. It was the paper Arnold had taken from the hem of his tunic. But it would hardly do to say so. "Why would I?"

"It's the same code you translated before," Gower said impatiently. "From the rebels' newspaper."

"Oh. Yes. I'm sorry. As I said, I'm not quite awake."

"Well, when you are, I want you to decipher it for me."

"Where did you get it?"

"One of our men intercepted it. The bearer was trying to deliver it to a man named Pedro O'Reilly—a rebel sympathizer." The colonel gave that thin smile of his again. "Unfortunately for him, we had already learned where O'Reilly's loyalties lay. He's now in prison."

"O'Reilly? Or the messenger?" Creighton tried not to sound as anxious as he felt.

"O'Reilly. The messenger managed to escape. But he shouldn't be difficult to find. Apparently he's an enormous fellow. Of course, the men who told me this may have exaggerated, to explain why they couldn't hold on to him."

"If they find him, will they . . . will they hang him?"

Gower made a disparaging noise. "Unfortunately, no. The governor's afraid that if we hang too many rebels, the colonists will make trouble. As a result, our prison is teeming with traitors."

"Including Washington, I suppose?" Creighton said, as casually as he could.

His uncle glanced at him sharply, as though wondering what purpose lay behind this question. But Creighton had his mask of innocence ready, and it seemed to satisfy the colonel. "No," he said. "Not Washington."

Creighton didn't think it wise to press the matter. He laid the coded message on his nightstand. "I'll work on this once I'm fully awake."

Gower rose from his chair. "Make it soon. I suspect it has something to do with the plan the Spanish and the Americans are hatching."

"Oh?"

"Arnold tells me they mean to attack our fort at Mobile within the week."

When the colonel was gone, Creighton collapsed on the bed, exhausted from his efforts. His mind was more muddled than ever, fairly humming with half-formed thoughts and questions and suspicions. He had known Arnold would give information to the British, but it was supposed to be false information. According to Peter, the Patriots and their allies really *were* going to attack Mobile. Why would Arnold reveal the actual plans, unless . . . unless he had truly turned his coat after all?

It was an unpleasant thought but, he had to admit, a credible one. Arnold had repeatedly expressed his disgust with the Patriots, with their inability to agree, their unwillingness to act. What was it Peter had said—that the general would prefer to fight for anything rather than for nothing? Despite Peter's low opinion of his own intelligence, sometimes the giant had a way of getting to the heart of things.

Arnold had also made it clear how much he disliked the Spanish and the French. If England was preparing to wage war on those countries, Arnold might welcome the chance to be part of it. The idea seemed very plausible to Creighton—and very disturbing. If Arnold couldn't be trusted, and Peter couldn't be found, where did that leave *him*?

He picked up the coded message and regarded it thoughtfully. He certainly wasn't about to translate it for his uncle's benefit. But perhaps he should translate it for his own enlightenment. It might tell him something more about Arnold's intentions. First, though, he had to find a copy of *The North American Almanac.* But even before that, he had to find something to take away the pain in his head.

It didn't take him long to locate an apothecary, who sold him a packet of headache powders. Locating the exact almanac he needed was more troublesome. Apparently it wasn't popular in Florida. Nearly every printing shop and confectioner's and tobacconist carried some sort of almanac. He found *Daboll's Almanac, Bickerstaff's Almanac,* and *Father Abraham's Almanac,* but not *The North American Almanac.*

At last it occurred to him that there was one place he was certain to find it: The Boar's Head Tavern. Even if Pedro O'Reilly had received the message, he couldn't have read it without the almanac as a key.

The prospect of deliberately walking into the very establishment where Peter had nearly been captured gave him pause. But no one would have any cause to suspect him. With his Bristol-bred speech and the presentable clothing provided by Hale—along with several shillings in spending money—he would give every appearance of being a member of the English gentry, not a Patriot spy.

The tavern was very much like the ones back home where he and the other wealthy wastrels had whiled away their nights. Creighton should have felt at ease there. Instead he felt curiously uneasy, out of his element. Had he changed so much, then, in these past few months? Even the ale, which had obviously been imported from England, tasted bitter on his tongue. And the idle louts who lounged about playing cards and laughing immoderately at one another's witticisms seemed to grate on him. Had his old companions been so loud, so full of themselves and so empty of substance?

Though he had no real desire for conversation, he took a seat across from a florid-faced man who was drinking something fruity smelling from a tankard and struck up a conversation about the weather. The man wasted no time in advancing what was clearly a cherished opinion—that this would be the hottest and driest summer ever seen, and that the crops would certainly wither and die, throwing all the southern colonies into economic ruin.

"That seems to me an unduly gloomy outlook," Creighton said. "In fact the predictions I've read call for a wetter, cooler summer than usual."

The man snorted derisively. "You must have been reading fairy tales, then."

"No, I assure you." Creighton turned and summoned the tavern keeper. "Would you happen to keep a copy of an almanac about? This gentleman and I wish to settle a small dispute."

"Well," said the tavern keeper, "that's better than settling it with pistols. I'm sure there's one somewhere."

"Bring me another ale, too, please, and another . . . whatever it is, for my friend."

"Shrub," said the florid-faced man.

"For Mr. Shrub."

The man laughed, spewing a bit of his drink onto the table. "No, no. My name's Hearne. Shrub is the drink—rum, mixed with pineapple, lemon, and spices."

"Ah. Well. I'll have the same, then."

The tavern keeper returned in a few minutes with the drinks and a copy of an almanac whose cover, to Creighton's relief, looked very familiar. "Now," Creighton said, "let's see what *The North American* has to say." As he briskly opened the pages of the almanac, his hand knocked over one of the tankards. Its fruity contents surged across the table and into the lap of Mr. Hearne, who stared dumbly at the deluge.

Creighton sprang to his feet, snatching the almanac out of harm's way. "Do forgive me, sir! So clumsy of me!"

"I'll clean it up," the tavern keeper said long-sufferingly.

"And I'll clean myself up," said Hearne irritably.

The moment they were gone, Creighton tossed two shillings onto the table, thrust the almanac inside his waistcoat, and strolled casually out the door.

When he entered the guardhouse, the door to Hale's room stood open. The lieutenant glanced up from a book in which he was jotting something. "There you are. Mr. Arnold came looking for you."

"What did he want?"

"He didn't say. Have you eaten?"

"What? Oh, yes." Actually, all he'd put in his stomach besides the headache powders and the ale were some salted herrings provided by the tavern to promote thirst. But he was less interested in food than in deciphering the coded message.

"What about a game of brag later on?" suggested Hale.

"Yes, fine," Creighton said absently. He went to his room and locked the door. He drew the almanac and the message from his waistcoat and set to work at once. Now that he had the key, the process was relatively swift and simple. Within an hour's time, he had printed on a separate scrap of paper:

AT DAWN SUNDAY NEXT FLEET OF AMERICAN FRENCH AND SPANISH VESSELS WILL ATTACK FORT AT 135 SINK OR DISABLE AS MANY ENGLISH VESSELS AS POSSIBLE IF ANY NEW INFORMATION REGARDING 46 PLEASE INFORM

The number 46, which had also appeared in *The Liberty Tree*'s coded passage, must refer to General Washington. The number 135 didn't seem to indicate a particular page, line, and word—unless the word was *diary,* which didn't seem likely. Creighton assumed it was also a substitute for a name—Mobile, no doubt.

Well, there was nothing in the message to either acquit Arnold or condemn him. Creighton folded the scrap of paper into a tiny square and, after a moment's consideration, swallowed it. Then he smoothed out the coded message and set about carefully composing a new and totally imaginary translation:

THE SONS OF LIBERTY COMMEND YOU FOR YOUR
EXCELLENT EFFORTS IN DISCOVERING THE LOCATION OF
THE GENERAL WE WILL MAKE CONTACT WITH THE
PRISONER AND ARRANGE HIS ESCAPE AT THE EARLIEST
POSSIBLE OPPORTUNITY

When he was finished, Creighton examined his handiwork critically. A bit wordy, but it should do the job.

Chapter TWENTY

*B*eing appointed lieutenant governor seemed to have made little difference in Colonel Gower's life, outwardly at least. The room into which Creighton was shown by the colonel's clerk was a bit larger than the one back in Carolina, and the furnishings were a bit more elegant, but there was the same air of impermanence about the place, as though the colonel didn't expect to stay long.

Gower was in his bedchamber, bent over the battered ironbound war chest. "What is it?" he called over his shoulder.

"I've deciphered the message, as you asked."

"Ah. Good." His uncle closed the chest and emerged from the bedchamber, carrying a walnut box with brass corners and hinges. He placed the box on his desk and held out a hand for the paper.

Though Creighton was sure Gower would suspect nothing, he couldn't keep his fingers from trembling slightly as he handed over his translation. He clasped his hands behind his back and tried to appear calm and confident while his uncle examined the counterfeit message. The colonel took an inordinate amount of time with it, as though he needed to go over it several times to make sense of it. At last he folded the paper slowly, deliberately, and raised his leaden eyes to Creighton. "Where is the key?"

"I beg your pardon?"

"The key," Gower repeated impatiently. "What you used to decipher the code. I want to see how you did it."

Creighton hesitated only a moment. "There is none. I merely substituted letters for numbers. It's a tedious process, with a lot of trial and error. That's why it took so long."

"Trial and error, eh?" The colonel unfolded the paper and surveyed it again. "I find it curious that there are so few erasures and corrections."

"I used a separate piece of paper for the trials and errors."

The colonel nodded. Then he said, rather amiably, "I don't believe you."

Creighton somehow contrived to make his voice sound indignant and not panicky. "Do you suppose I made all that up?" He snatched the paper angrily from his uncle's hand and waved it about. "You ask me to decipher it, so I rack my brain for hours on end, despite the constant pain in my head, and *this* is the thanks I get?"

The colonel seemed amused at this outburst. "You always were good at feigning injury. When you were a small boy, I once gave you a slap on the wrist for pulling at my wig. You howled as though I'd broken something, and wouldn't leave off until your mother bribed you with sweetmeats." Gower glanced at the clock on the mantelpiece. "I'd call your bluff, and have you demonstrate for me exactly how you came up with that . . . *dubious* message, but I haven't the time. I have an appointment shortly, one that I must keep."

He turned to the box, unfastened the brass clasp, and lifted the lid. Inside, couched in red velvet, was a brace of ornate dueling pistols with walnut stocks and brass butt plates. "We will resume our discussion when I return." He took up one of the pistols and wiped the oil from its barrel with a cloth. "Presuming, of course, that I *do* return."

"You're going to fight a duel?"

The colonel gave him a disdainful look. "You always were quick to grasp the obvious, too."

"With whom?" Creighton asked, though he had the unpleasant feeling that he knew the answer.

"With your compatriot, Mr. Arnold."

"Arnold? Why?"

Gower held the pistol at arm's length and sighted down the barrel. "I accused him of being a spy. He took offense, and challenged me."

"But—but why would you accuse him? When we spoke this morning, you seemed satisfied that he could be trusted."

"That was before he began quizzing me about Washington—much the way you had just done." Gower cocked the hammer of the flintlock and pulled the trigger. Creighton flinched as the flint struck the frizzen, sending up a small shower of sparks.

"I didn't *quiz* you about Washington. I merely wondered what had become of him."

"Well, perhaps you should ask the person who wrote *that*." The colonel waved the pistol at the paper in Creighton's hand. "Apparently he knows. Assuming, of course, that what you've printed there is the actual message, and not just a sham, designed to trick me into revealing Washington's whereabouts."

"You're implying that I'm a spy, too, and I resent it!"

"Do you? Then perhaps you should challenge me as well. I could accommodate you in . . ." He consulted the clock again. "Say, half an hour, when I've done with Arnold. Oh, by the by . . . I believe he wishes you to be his second. I've chosen Hale as mine, if you'd be so good as to inform him."

"You're making a mistake!" Creighton said desperately. "Arnold is no spy, nor am I!"

Gower shrugged. "Even if that were so, it would make no difference. It's a question of honor, now."

"You'd kill a man, or be killed yourself, for no reason?"

"Satisfying one's honor is reason enough. Without his honor, a gentleman has nothing. Did your father never teach you that?"

"No," Creighton said grimly. "He taught me that without his *life*, a gentleman has nothing."

The colonel turned that wolfish gaze on him again. "When a man turns traitor," he said pointedly, "he forfeits both his life and his honor."

"What my father did was not treason!" Creighton fought back the tears that stung his eyes. "What he did was *right*!"

For the first time that Creighton could recall, his uncle's face registered surprise. "You know what truly became of him, then?"

"Yes!" Creighton hissed. "And I know what your part in it was!" He backed toward the door. "I'll be Arnold's second, willingly. And I hope to God that he shoots straight through your black heart!"

Creighton had never had occasion to participate in a duel, either as a principal or as a second. But he knew the procedures and the unwritten code of honor that governed them, from listening to the knights of the tavern recount their exploits. All of them had fought or seconded in at least one duel.

Thomas Kern had once agreed to be a second for his cousin, only to find himself shooting it out with the opponent's second, who insisted that his cousin's misfire must count as a shot. After firing three totally ineffectual shots apiece, they had reconciled, and so had the two principals.

Aside from Roger Davy, whose smallest finger had been shot off, none had suffered a serious wound. The acknowledged purpose of dueling was, after all, not to kill your opponent, but to satisfy your honor and his. In minor disputes, combatants had been known to "dumb fire," or discharge their weapons into the air, so as not to risk actually harming one another.

But that was the English way of dueling. Americans seemed less concerned with honor than they were with winning, by whatever means necessary.

Hale was apparently well acquainted with duels, too. "It's up to the colonel to pick the weapons," he said, "as well as the time and place. Obviously he's chosen pistols. Did he say when or where they'd meet?"

"He didn't say where. He said something about half an hour—and that was ten minutes ago."

"Well, there's only one place here where duels are fought—Gage Hill." Hale shook his head. "I wish they'd waited until morning, as the *code duello* requires. It'd be easier to talk them out of it if they had a chance to cool down."

"Neither one is going to apologize or back down, no matter how long they wait or what we say."

"Probably not. But it's our duty as seconds to try."

The lieutenant was right. Though the colonel might deserve to be shot, it would serve no purpose; it wouldn't bring back Creighton's father—or Franklin. As for Arnold, if he had betrayed the Patriots, then he, too, deserved whatever he got. But Creighton still couldn't be certain whose side the man was on. He sighed. "In that case," he said, "we'd better hurry."

When they reached the top of Gage Hill, both men were waiting. Arnold was pacing about impatiently; Gower leaned nonchalantly against a tree with the box of pistols at his feet.

"I didn't bring powder or bullets," Hale whispered. "That should delay things a bit." But as they drew nearer, they saw that the colonel had also brought an ammunition case and a powder horn. "So much for that," Hale muttered. "Go see if you can reason with your man. I'll talk to mine—for all the good it'll do."

Creighton approached the general; before he could speak, Arnold said, "Why didn't you tell me he was your uncle?"

"I didn't think you'd trust me, if you knew."

"You have no qualms about seconding me, against him?"

"None. But are you sure you want to go through with this?"

"If I don't, it's as much as admitting that I'm a spy."

Creighton leaned in closer and said softly, "You *are* a spy." The question was, for which side?

"Gower doesn't know that. He's only guessing."

"Well, I don't see how killing him—or getting yourself killed—is going to change his mind."

"The fact that I'm willing to fight may convince him that he accused me unjustly."

"And what if it doesn't?"

Arnold shrugged. "One way or the other, he won't be able to accuse me again."

When Hale and Creighton met again in the center of the field, the lieutenant was carrying the pistols, the powder, and the ammunition case. "I take it you couldn't talk him out of it," Creighton said.

Hale shook his head. "And you?"

"No."

"Well." Hale handed one of the pistols to Creighton. "Is that weapon all right with you? The colonel says he likes the balance of this one better."

Creighton looked the pistol over. "I don't suppose it matters."

"Probably not, but—" Hale moved nearer and murmured, "Check it carefully anyway, lad." He raised his eyebrows significantly.

Creighton blinked in puzzlement, and glanced toward the colonel. "You—you don't think he'd—"

"I don't think anything. I'm just saying, check it carefully, eh?"

Creighton tested the hammer; it moved freely. He checked the screw that held the flint in place; it was tight. He examined the touch hole and the inside of the barrel; they were clean.

"You know how to load it?" the lieutenant asked.

"Of course. We practiced marksmanship in school." Creighton poured a charge of powder down the barrel, wrapped a lead ball in a paper wad and pushed it into place with the ramrod, then primed the pan with a little powder.

Hale nodded approvingly. "That's got it." He cast a glance around the field. "How does twenty paces sound to you? They're less likely to hit each other than they would be at ten."

"All right, I suppose."

"The colonel prefers to fire at pleasure, not at a signal. Any objections?"

Creighton's throat seemed too dry and tight to answer, so he simply shook his head. Hale held out his hand and Creighton grasped it limply; the feeling seemed to have deserted his fingers. "Good luck to your man," the lieutenant said.

Creighton started to say, "And to yours," but then he hesitated and frowned.

"What is it?" Hale said.

"It's just that . . . it doesn't seem right, wishing one person luck in shooting another."

"I wasn't. I was wishing him luck in not *getting* shot."

"Oh," Creighton said. "Good luck to your man, too, then."

When the colonel had taken up his position, Hale measured off twenty paces and showed Arnold where to stand. Then he stepped out of the line of fire and called, "At your pleasure, gentlemen!"

The colonel turned sideways, as a swordsman does, to offer as small a target as possible. Arnold chose to face his opponent head-on. Both men raised their weapons and cocked them. Before either had time to aim properly, the colonel's pistol discharged with a puff of smoke and a sharp report.

Arnold gave a grunt of pain and staggered slightly, but quickly recovered. His face drawn and grim, he took aim and squeezed the trigger of his weapon. Though the hammer fell on the frizzen, there was no smoke and no sound—nothing. With a curse, Arnold lowered the pistol and examined it. His left arm was clamped tightly to his side; beneath it, a red stain was spreading across the fabric of his coat.

The colonel had calmly set about reloading his pistol. "Wait!" Creighton cried. "There's a problem with his weapon!" Gower ignored him. "Lieutenant Hale! Will you stop your man?"

"Your man's misfire counts as a shot," Hale said regretfully. "He'll have to reload."

"How can he reload if his weapon hasn't fired?" Creighton hurried over to Arnold, who was still trying to find the problem. "I loaded it correctly! I'm certain of it!" Creighton glanced toward the colonel. Gower had finished loading and was raising the pistol for another shot. "No!" Creighton stepped in front of Arnold. "Give him a moment! There's something wrong!"

"I always said you were useless!" Gower shouted. "You can't even load a pistol properly! Stand aside now, or I'll put a ball through your empty head!"

"I won't!" Creighton flung his arms wide, inviting Gower to shoot him. The colonel hesitated, obviously uncertain for once what to do. Then an arm pushed Creighton roughly out of the way. He fell on to one knee. Before he could recover he heard two reports, almost on top of each other, one at a distance and one close at hand.

He sprang to his feet, glancing frantically from Arnold to his uncle and back again. For a moment neither man moved; it seemed that both shots had missed their mark. Then the colonel's shooting arm went limp and the pistol fell from his grasp. Slowly he sank to his knees and then, just as slowly, sagged sideways. Hale caught him before he struck the ground.

Creighton turned to Arnold. As the man lowered his pistol, Creighton saw to his astonishment that it wasn't the same weapon that had misfired. This was a plainer model, with a steel butt plate and a stock made of oak. The more ornate pistol lay in the grass at his feet. "Where did—how did you—"

"I had it beneath my coat," Arnold said. "Prepare for the worst, remember?" He bent over, grimacing with pain, and retrieved the fallen pistol. "The misfire was not due to anything you did or didn't do." He pulled back the hammer and ran a finger along the face of the frizzen. "Someone has coated this with a thin layer of clear varnish so it won't strike a spark."

"My uncle," Creighton murmured. Feeling unsteady, almost dizzy, he covered the twenty paces to where the colonel lay and knelt beside him. The man's head hung limp; his eyes were closed; his breathing was labored and rasping. A trickle of blood issued from the corner of his mouth.

Gower seemed to sense Creighton's presence and languidly opened his eyes. Though he was clearly trying to speak, no sound came out. One hand was pressed to the side of his chest; when he raised it, he revealed a neat, blood-ringed hole in his waistcoat. Creighton guessed that because of his uncle's sideways stance, the ball had passed though both of his lungs. Gower beckoned weakly to him.

Creighton leaned over until his ear was a few inches from the man's mouth. The colonel uttered something that was scarcely more than a sigh. Then his eyes closed again and his head lolled backward. Arnold crouched and placed two fingers on the colonel's throat, feeling for a pulse. Then he shook his head. "He's gone." Creighton got to his feet and stood looking about, feeling dazed and dreamlike. Arnold rose and placed a hand on his shoulder, but Creighton pulled away, wanting no comfort, especially from someone who might be no more trustworthy than his uncle had been.

Arnold turned to Hale. "What did the colonel say?"

"I couldn't hear," the lieutenant replied.

Creighton put a hand to his head, which had begun to throb again. He had heard Gower's last words clearly enough, but he wasn't certain that he understood them, or that he should divulge them to either of these men. What the colonel had said was, "St. Marks. Number four."

Chapter TWENTY-ONE

Lieutenant Hale lowered the colonel's body onto the grass and stood. "I'll have to let the governor know. If I were you, I wouldn't stay around to see what he does about it."

"Why should I leave?" Arnold said. "I've done nothing wrong."

"They have laws here against dueling. Usually the governor looks the other way, but considering that it's his lieutenant governor, and considering he's dead . . ."

"I suppose you're right. Will you give me an hour's start before you inform anyone?"

Hale considered a moment, then nodded. "One hour."

Arnold beckoned to Creighton. "Come." Creighton hesitated, and then, not knowing what else to do, went with him. "I don't like to leave," Arnold said, "without having learned anything about Washington."

"You should have thought of that before you challenged the colonel. Besides—" Creighton broke off, still unsure how far he could trust Arnold.

"What?"

"Nothing." He glanced at the general's bloody coat. "Shouldn't we tend to that wound?"

"It can wait."

"Where will we go now?"

"Back to New Orleans. I had hoped to free Washington before the attack on Pensacola. I'm afraid the British might kill him just to keep him out of our hands."

"Pensacola? I thought the attack was to be on Mobile!"

"The plans changed. I only told Gower that so he would send his troops there and leave Pensacola unprotected."

"Oh. But—why didn't you tell me this before?"

"There was no need for you to know. Besides . . . I wasn't certain I could trust you."

"Not *trust* me?"

"Well, you are English, after all."

"Only by birth." Creighton was silent a moment, then said, "What does the number 135 mean?"

"It's our code for Pensacola. Why?"

"And what does the number 46 mean?"

"It's the code for Washington. Why do you ask?"

"And what does St. Marks, number four mean?"

Arnold gave him an exasperated glance. "St. Marks is a British fort, fifty miles or so east of here."

"Do they have a prison?"

"Probably, but—"

"Then number four could be a cell number?"

"I suppose," Arnold said impatiently. "Why?"

"Those were the last words my uncle spoke. I thought he might be telling us where to find Washington."

"Why would he do that?"

"I don't know. Perhaps it's his way of atoning for his sins. Besides, what else could it mean?"

Arnold didn't reply. They walked on in silence until they reached the State House, then Arnold halted. "I have a task for you. Go to your uncle's quarters. Bring back his spare uniform, and the official seal he keeps in his desk."

Creighton gave him a puzzled look. "Why?"

"I can't explain now."

"I thought you trusted me."

"If I didn't, I wouldn't ask you to do this, would I?" He handed Creighton a small brass key. "For the desk."

"Where did you get this?"

"From his waistcoat pocket, when I bent over him just now. We'll meet at the dock, where we left the dinghy, in half an hour."

"Where are you going?"

"To get my ribs bandaged, and then to fetch Peter."

"Oh. I never told you. They caught Peter trying to deliver the message to O'Reilly."

Arnold cursed softly. "Where is he now?"

"I don't know. He got away, but they may have apprehended him by now."

"Perhaps not. Peter is more clever than he lets on. I'll see what I can learn. Half an hour, at the dock."

Creighton wanted to ask how he was supposed to make off with the colonel's uniform and seal without attracting suspicion, but Arnold was already gone. He took a deep breath and headed for the State House. Peter wasn't the only one who could be clever.

He strode into the colonel's antechamber as though he owned it and nodded to the young clerk. "My uncle sent me to fetch his spare uniform. It needs to be cleaned and pressed for the ball tomorrow night."

"Ball?" the clerk said. "There's to be a ball? No one told me."

"Nine o'clock, at the governor's mansion," Creighton called over his shoulder as he disappeared into the colonel's quarters. Swiftly he detoured to the desk, which was out of the clerk's sight. The state seal lay in the very first drawer he unlocked. He pocketed it, then moved on to the bedchamber just as the clerk appeared in the doorway.

"I wonder why I wasn't invited," the fellow said rather forlornly.

"I couldn't say." Creighton lifted the colonel's uniform from the wardrobe. As an afterthought, he snatched up a blanket, too. "Would you like me to get an invitation for you?"

"Could you?" the clerk said, then added confidentially, "I have my eye on the governor's daughter, you know!"

Creighton patted his shoulder. "Good for you. Aim high, that's what I always say. I'll have that invitation for you by tomorrow morning." He winked broadly. "Don't tell anyone, eh?"

"Not a word," the clerk vowed. "Thank you!"

"Don't mention it." Once outside, Creighton rolled the uniform up in the blanket, then proceeded to the docks. There was no sign of Arnold. He climbed into the dinghy. The sun had dropped behind the buildings now, and the mosquitoes were coming out. Creighton unwrapped the uniform and draped the blanket over himself for protection.

Just before the light drained entirely from the sky, Arnold appeared at the end of the dock, carrying a bundle under one arm. He lowered himself into the boat and untied it from its mooring.

"You didn't find Peter, I take it."

The general shook his head. "We'll have to leave without him."

"We can't!" Creighton protested. "They know he's a spy! It's only a matter of time before they catch him!"

Arnold sat down and took up the oars. "And if we stay, they'll have three prisoners instead of one." He pushed the dinghy away from the dock and began to row toward the sloop in the harbor. "I'm sorry, but Peter knew the risks involved. He'll understand."

"I'm relieved that someone does," Creighton said, "because I don't. I don't see why things that are considered unacceptable or immoral in ordinary life—killing, treachery . . . deserting your friends—somehow become acceptable when they're performed in the name of a cause."

"They don't become acceptable," Arnold replied. "But they do become necessary. War reduces us to the necessities. We can no longer afford such luxuries as conscience and compassion."

Creighton stared at the dark figure silhouetted against the water. The general's words reminded him of something his uncle had said, about how his father had let his judgment be impaired by compassion. At the time, he hadn't understood what Gower meant; now he thought perhaps he did understand.

He had always believed, growing up, that countries—or at least *his* country—waged war according to an unwritten code of honor, like the one that governed dueling. Now he realized how it really worked: When two opponents—or two armies, or two different ways of life or thought—met and clashed, then rules and ideals and honor were left behind, along with homes and families.

As they neared the sloop, Creighton fancied he saw a shadowy shape appear momentarily at the starboard rail, then merge again with the other shadows. "I think there's someone aboard!" he called softly, over the splash of the oars.

Arnold shipped the oars and, reaching beneath his coat, drew out the pistol. The dinghy bumped gently against the hull of the sloop. Arnold signaled to Creighton to tie the boat fast, then hoisted himself over the rail. Creighton waited tensely for the sound of a struggle, or a cry, or a shot. There was nothing. Growing anxious, he stood on the seat of the dinghy and peered over the gunwales of the sloop.

"It's all right," a voice said, nearly in his ear, severely startling him. "It's just me."

"Peter?" Creighton climbed aboard. "How did you get out here?"

"Swam," the giant said.

"I'm glad to see you. We feared you'd been taken."

Peter laughed. "I'm not that easily captured."

"Hoist the dinghy and the anchor," Arnold called, "and we'll get under way."

"To where?" Peter asked.

"St. Marks."

"St. Marks?" Peter whispered to Creighton. "What's there?"

"Well," Creighton replied, "we're hoping that General Washington is."

They reached Apalachee Bay, where St. Marks was situated, the following afternoon. Arnold raised the Union Jack atop the mast, then handed Creighton the bundle he had brought aboard. "Put that on."

Creighton unwrapped it. It was a British corporal's uniform. "Where did this come from?"

"The guardhouse."

"Didn't its owner object?"

"As I recall, his exact words were, 'Take it, take it, just don't shoot.' "

As Creighton was getting into the unfortunate corporal's coat, something pricked his ribs. Deep in an inside pocket he discovered a small dagger, the sort soldiers used for cutting up meat and bread—and, in a quarrel, one another. He shifted it to a more comfortable spot.

Arnold, meanwhile, had donned Colonel Gower's uniform. "I'm sorry I couldn't find one for you," he told Peter. "You know how it is."

"I know." The giant gave a sigh of resignation.

Arnold disappeared into the sloop's cabin and emerged half an hour later, carrying an official-looking document sealed with wax that bore the impression of the seal of West Florida. "Orders from the governor," he explained as he tucked the paper inside his coat, "authorizing us to transport the prisoner to Pensacola."

"Do you think they'll believe it?" Creighton asked.

"I'm sure they will," Arnold said. "Unless, of course, they don't."

St. Marks could hardly be called a proper settlement; there was nothing there but a limestone fort, a tavern, a few warehouses, and half a dozen dwellings. They dropped anchor in the bay, and Creighton and Arnold stepped into the dinghy. "Good luck," Peter said wistfully.

"You'll do the rowing," the general told Creighton. "No self-respecting British officer would stoop to such a menial task. The Brits put a lot of stock in appearances; if we look as though we know what we're doing, they'll assume we do."

"You don't have a very high opinion of my . . . my *former* countrymen, do you?"

"They've given me no reason to."

"Well, it's a pity you never met my father."

"Was he anything like your uncle?"

Creighton laughed. "God, no. He was good-humored, and kind, and patient—even with me."

"Really?" Arnold said. "He must have been extraordinary, then."

Creighton glanced sharply at the general, wondering whether he was jesting or not. Arnold gave no sign one way or the other. "Speaking of my uncle, are you putting on his identity as well as his uniform?"

"No. I'll use my own name. Someone here may have fought against me, and might recognize me."

"And if they do?"

He shrugged. "I've changed my loyalties, remember?"

The sentry at the gate clearly put his faith in appearances. When Arnold approached, he came to attention and saluted so vigorously that it knocked his hat awry. "Sir!" Arnold returned the salute with an indifferent air befitting an arrogant British officer.

"Colonel Arnold," Creighton said briskly, "to see the commandant."

"I'll have to ask you to leave any weapons here, sir," the guard said apologetically. "Captain's orders."

Arnold hesitated, then withdrew the pistol he had concealed beneath his coat. "That's all I have." The guard took him at his word, but wasn't so trusting with a mere corporal. He patted Creighton's clothing briskly and then, satisfied that he was unarmed, said, "Follow me, sir!" He led them through the gate and across the parade ground to the officers' quarters, where he handed them over to a clerk. The clerk in turn showed them into the commandant's chambers. The youthful commandant, a mere captain, fairly leaped from his chair in his eagerness to greet his high-ranking guest. "How may I assist you, sir?"

Arnold handed over the sealed document. "His Excellency has instructed me to collect a rebel prisoner you're holding here."

"Oh? What prisoner?"

"He didn't inform me. I presume that information is in the orders."

The captain broke the seal and perused the writing inside. His expression changed abruptly from eager to troubled. "It—it says here that he wants Washington."

"Is that a problem?"

Frowning, the captain read the letter again, as though to be certain he'd understood it properly. "Well . . . yes, actually. You see, I've only just assumed command here, and, frankly, I've no idea what the man looks like, or what cell he's in. There's undoubtedly a list of prisoners here, somewhere . . ." He began rummaging through the pile of papers on his desk.

"I was told he would be in cell number four."

"Ah. Number four, is it?" The captain put the document in his desk, then took his sword belt and hat down from the wall and put them on. "I'll accompany you."

They crossed the parade ground again and descended a set of steps into a stone cellar, where rows of heavy wooden doors reinforced with iron lined a cobbled corridor. One of the doors stood ajar, revealing a guard stretched out on a bunk, sound asleep. The commandant scowled and shook the man roughly. "Get up, Private."

Yawning, the guard got to his feet and saluted lazily. "It's Sergeant, sir."

"Not any longer. Which is cell number four?"

"Why, the fourth one, sir."

"Open it."

"Yes, sir." He shuffled to one of the massive doors, turned an iron key in the lock, and with some effort, pushed open the door. The captain gestured for them to enter. "Your prisoner, sir."

"I hope he's in good health." Arnold stepped through the doorway, and Creighton followed.

The cell was not as cramped or as dismal as he'd feared, but neither was it fit quarters for a captured officer, particularly a general. The room was poorly lighted by a small window, barred with iron, set above eye level so that all that could be seen through it was a square of sky. When Creighton's eyes adjusted to the gloom, he saw that the furnishings consisted of a desk, a chair, and a narrow bunk. It was a moment before he noticed the figure huddled in the corner, at the head of the bunk.

He had expected the prisoner to be in uniform. Instead the man wore an ordinary shirt and breeches, a bit tattered but reasonably clean. When they entered, the man was curled into a ball, his arms wrapped about his legs, his head slumped forward onto his knees. Now he raised his countenance to them slowly, apathetically, as though he had little interest in learning who his visitors were.

His face was clean-shaven and his hair had been recently trimmed, not very neatly. It was difficult to make out his features in the dim light. Arnold stepped forward and peered into the man's face. "Damn!" he said softly. "It's not Washington!"

"Not Washington?" Creighton echoed in dismay. "Then who?"

Arnold crouched down before the prisoner. "What's your name, man?" The prisoner gazed at him blankly, as though he were speaking a foreign tongue. "Are you American?"

The man shook his head almost imperceptibly. "English," he said. His voice was faint and hoarse.

"What's your name? Can you tell me your name?"

The reply was so feeble that Creighton could scarcely hear, but he could have sworn that the man said, "Brown. Harry Brown."

Chapter TWENTY-TWO

*W*hen Creighton was younger and indulged in frequent displays of temper, a physician had blamed it on a surfeit of blood and recommended regular bloodletting. They had had to hold Creighton down to perform the procedure. Afterward his limbs had felt so weak and useless that he could scarcely stand, but he had forced himself to, just to show them that he couldn't be ruled so easily.

His limbs felt the same now—as though all the strength had drained from them. But he forced himself forward and bent to examine the prisoner's face. It wasn't the same face he remembered. The cheeks were sunken; the blue eyes were nearly hidden behind drooping eyelids; the sallow skin was marred by open sores. Still, it was familiar enough to make his heart leap with hope. He could scarcely bear to say the word in his mind, for fear the man would deny it: "Father?"

The prisoner turned his dull gaze on Creighton. "Who?"

Fighting back tears, Creighton clutched the man's hand and shook it, like a small child desperate to get a parent's attention. "It's me, Father!" he said, in a voice so thick and strange he hardly recognized it as his own. "It's Creighton!"

"Creighton?" the man whispered, and his eyes widened in recognition, or disbelief. "Here?"

The moment was shattered by a hollow booming sound that filled the cell. Creighton spun about to see that the heavy door had swung closed. Arnold strode across the cell and shouted through the small opening in the door, "Guard! Open this at once!"

The commandant's face appeared in the opening. He no longer appeared eager or solicitous. "What?" he said, in mock surprise. "You didn't find the man you were seeking?"

"No. I'd like to examine the other cells."

"I'm afraid it would prove entirely fruitless, since your General Washington isn't here. He's in the graveyard, buried beneath a plain wooden cross. You see, he was hanged, not long after his arrival here."

Arnold thrust one hand through the opening, reaching for the captain's throat. The man stepped nimbly aside and, seizing Arnold's wrist, rammed it viciously against the side of the opening. "Who sent you here?" he demanded.

Though Arnold's face was distorted by pain, he managed to make his voice indignant and imperious. "Governor Chester, you imbecile! And he'll have you flogged and stripped of your rank for this!"

The captain released his hold on Arnold's wrist. "The governor is well aware of Washington's fate, since he ordered it. Why would he send you to fetch a dead man?"

"He didn't indicate whether we'd find Washington dead or alive, he merely said to bring him back, and I intend to do so."

"And I intend to keep you safely locked up until I can determine the truth of the matter. I'm sure the governor won't mind waiting a few more days. After all, Washington won't be going anywhere." He gave a smug smile. "And neither will you." His face disappeared from the opening.

Arnold raised one foot and delivered a kick that made the door rattle in its frame. Then he turned away and began pacing about the room, rubbing his injured forearm. "A pox on the man! Why did we have to encounter the one British officer in a thousand who thinks for himself?"

Creighton sank down on the bunk next to his father and put his aching head in his hands. "I'm sorry, Father. We should have freed you; instead, it looks as though we'll join you."

For a moment Harry Brown didn't respond; he seemed not to have heard. Then slowly, hesitantly, like someone recalling an old habit long forgotten and long unpracticed, he raised his arm and laid it tentatively across his son's shoulders. "You did your best," he murmured.

Creighton leaned into him, and for the first time since he'd learned of his father's supposed death two years before, he let a breach open in the wall of anger and insolence he had built to contain the grief, the way the earthen wall at New Orleans held back the river, and the tears found their way through, in a trickle at first, then in a rush.

When the flood of emotion began to ebb, Creighton replaced it with a deluge of questions that, as it soon became obvious to him, his father was unable to answer. In his relief at seeing Harry Brown alive, Creighton had overlooked the fact that the man was desperately ill. One moment he was sweating and flushed with fever, the next he was gripped by chills so violent that his teeth chattered.

"Malaria, I have no doubt," said Arnold. "I wonder if they've given him Peruvian bark." He strode to the door again and shouted for the guard, but there was no response.

"We have to get him out," Creighton said, "and very soon."

"I know that. If you have any suggestions as to how, I'd be glad to hear them." Arnold dragged the desk beneath the window and, standing atop it, examined the iron bars. "They're well rusted, and the mortar is crumbling in places, but it would take several days to work one loose, even if we had a tool to work with." The general stepped down and pushed the desk back to its place.

Creighton dug into his coat pocket and came up with the small dagger, which had escaped the guard's notice. "Prepare for the worst, remember?" he said wryly. He handed the knife to Arnold, who tested its point.

"This should do. We'll have to wait until after dark to try it, though."

Between bouts of chills and fever, Harry Brown experienced fairly lengthy lucid spells. Though his body and his voice were weak, he managed some brief bits of conversation. When Creighton told him how he'd been treated by his uncle, and how the colonel had met his end, his father said, "Don't judge him too harshly. When I was court-martialed for 'aiding the enemy,' he spoke up in my defense. It was his intervention that saved me from the rope."

"But why did he lie to us, and say you'd died in battle?"

"To spare you the shame of knowing that I was a traitor, I suppose."

"I wouldn't have been ashamed."

His father smiled faintly. "You say that now. But you've changed. I'll wager that your mother would see things differently, eh?"

Creighton nodded reluctantly. "Still, she'll be glad to learn that you're alive."

Harry Brown gave a feeble laugh that dissolved into a fit of coughing. "Barely," he said at last.

Creighton swallowed hard and forced himself to look confident. "We'll find a way out of here, and we'll take you with us."

"Good." He patted Creighton's hand with his own, which was nearly as clammy and rough as the stones of the cell. "But I want you to promise me something: When that time comes, if I'm too weak to travel, you're to go without me. I want your word on it."

Uncertain how to reply, Creighton glanced at Arnold. The general nodded slightly. "You have my word," Creighton said.

As soon as the square of sky turned dark, they shoved the desk under the window again and took turns chipping with the dagger at the mortar around the base of the bars. On the outside, the window lay at ground level. It looked out on the parade ground, which was surrounded by a high stone wall. Every few yards or so there was an opening in the wall through which the barrels of cannon protruded, aiming at the bay. Above the cannon ports was a wooden walkway, where two sentries circled the perimeter in opposite directions. Every quarter hour or so, one of the sentries came so near their window that they had to leave off working until he was out of earshot.

By the time they had dug out the mortar to a depth of an inch or so, Creighton's hands were aching and his palms were blistered. When Arnold took his place at the window, he climbed down and sagged onto the chair. "This will take forever," he groaned. "What are we going to do?"

"Be quiet!" Arnold whispered. "Listen!"

Creighton climbed up next to him and put one ear to the window. "I don't hear anything."

"Exactly. No sentry. It's been more than a quarter hour since the last one."

"Perhaps they're just changing the watch."

"No. The Brits invariably divide the watch into four-hour shifts. They changed less than two hours ago."

"Look!" Creighton pointed to an indistinct form moving toward them, nearly invisible in the shadows at the base of the wall.

"I don't see anything," Arnold said.

The shape disappeared, and Creighton began to think that he'd only imagined it. Then he heard a faint voice from somewhere outside. "Creighton? General Arnold?"

Arnold grasped the bars as though he meant to pull them out bare-handed. "Peter! Over here!"

A moment later Peter's great form blocked out the sky. "Thank God! When you didn't come back, I thought something must've gone wrong. Looks like I was right."

"How did you get inside the walls?" Arnold asked.

"With a rope and a grappling hook."

"I hope you brought weapons."

"I took the muskets from the sentries—after I'd clobbered 'em, of course."

"Hand them through."

"I've got a better idea, sir. Stand back." Abruptly, he vanished from sight again.

"What's he up to?" Creighton wondered.

"I'm not sure," Arnold said as he descended from the desk. "But you'd best do as he says."

Puzzled, Creighton peered between the bars, searching for some sign of Peter. There was a sudden rumbling sound, like thunder, and a moment later an immense black shape came lumbering out of the dark, heading straight for him. With a cry, he stumbled backward, off the edge of the desk, and landed painfully on his backside on the stones.

Like a crack of lightning following the thunder, there was a tremendous clash of iron on iron. The bars that blocked the window sprang free from their sockets; one flew across the cell, narrowly missing Creighton's head.

The square of charcoal-colored sky was blotted out momentarily by an even darker cylindrical shape. Then, with a screech of metal, it withdrew from the opening, to be replaced by Peter's head. "Come on!" he called. "Hurry!"

Creighton heard a clamor of footsteps and voices from the corridor. It wouldn't take the guards long to determine which cell had been broken into. He snatched up the bar that had nearly impaled him, thrust one end between the stones of the floor, and jammed the other end against the door.

Arnold had already scrambled through the window, and was holding out a hand to him. "Quickly!"

"Wait!" Creighton lunged to the bunk and yanked his father's shivering form into a sitting position.

"No!" his father protested feebly. "Leave—" But his words were cut off, along with his breath, as Creighton thrust one shoulder into the man's midsection, lifted him from the bunk, and staggered toward the window.

Though Harry Brown's wasted frame was lighter than he had expected, Creighton couldn't manage to hoist both himself and his father onto the desk. "Help me, here!" he called out breathlessly.

"I've got him!" Peter's voice replied, and a second later the burden of his father's body was pulled from his back and through the window. Before Creighton could muster the strength to follow, he heard the rattle of the guard's key in the lock, and then the sound of something heavy pounding on the door. "The devil!" someone shouted. "They've wedged it shut!"

Spurred on by fear, Creighton clambered onto the desk and thrust his torso through the opening. "Halt!" ordered a voice behind him. Creighton's feet scrabbled at the stones, unable to find a purchase. Peter took hold of his arms, but before he could pull Creighton free, the guard had thrust his pistol through the opening in the door and fired. Creighton cried out as something struck his left leg, sending pain coursing through it.

As effortlessly as though Creighton were a child, Peter hauled him out onto the ground. As Arnold helped him to his feet, Creighton said, almost apologetically, "I'm shot."

"Can you walk?"

"I think so."

Peter slung Harry Brown over one shoulder like a sack of grain and headed for the wall. "We'll have to get out the same way I got in."

Hobbling after him, Creighton nearly collided with the cannon that Peter had used as a battering ram. Normally two men and a set of pulleys were required to maneuver a gun that size, but Peter had somehow managed not only to move it but to get it rolling with enough force to break through the bars. Creighton shook his head and thanked the heavens that the giant was on their side.

They clambered up the steps to the wooden walkway. Peter halted, looking around uncertainly. "Now where's that rope?" he muttered.

Across the parade ground, the door to the barracks burst open and a dozen half-clothed soldiers stumbled out, carrying lanterns and muskets. "You'd best find it quickly," Arnold said.

Peter groped along the top of the battlements with one hand, searching for the grappling hook. "It's here somewhere, it's here somewhere."

Creighton saw the flash of muskets from the ground below, like giant fireflies. An instant later he heard the reports; a ball ricocheted off the stones a foot away from him. Frantically he began running his hands along the wall, too, until they struck something metal. "Here it is!"

"Go on over!" Arnold told him.

"I can't! My leg!"

The general strode to him and, bending over, clasped his hands together. "Give me your foot."

Creighton raised his good leg and planted his foot in the general's hands. Arnold heaved him upward. With a shout of pain Creighton flung the wounded leg over the top of the wall, seized the rope, and half slid, half climbed down the outside of the wall. When he hit the ground, his leg crumpled beneath him and he went rolling down the slope. By the time he stopped himself and got to his feet, Arnold had reached the ground and Peter was descending the rope, still with Harry Brown draped across his broad back.

More musket flashes lit up the embrasures on the battlements above them. They scrambled downhill toward the bay, musket balls whining around them, sounding so much like mosquitoes—particularly large and deadly ones—that Creighton, out of old habit, flung his arms about, trying to wave them away.

He and Peter piled into the dinghy. While Arnold pushed them off, Creighton took up the oars. The moment Arnold was aboard, he began pulling for the sloop as though their lives depended on it—which they well might. As they were hoisting the dinghy over the rail of the ship, he heard an outbreak of thumping and clattering from the shore. "They're sending a boat after us!" he shouted.

"Raise the anchor, quickly," Arnold said.

After stretching Harry Brown out on the deck, Peter hurried forward to help Creighton with the heavy cast-iron anchor. Arnold set about raising the sails, but there was barely a breath of wind to fill them. "We'll never get under way in time!" Peter said. He lunged to the swivel gun that was mounted in the bow, then turned back, arms spread helplessly. "I've got no gunner's match to fire it with!"

Creighton peered over the rail. A longboat filled with soldiers from the fort was skimming toward them, only fifty yards away and closing in fast. "We'll have to fight them off!" he said grimly, and drew the small dagger, which was now dull from digging out mortar.

"I've got a better weapon than that!" Peter bent, took hold of the massive anchor, and with one heave, hoisted it over his head. As the longboat pulled alongside them, he stepped to the rail and flung the anchor overboard. With shouts of dismay, the sailors scattered. The anchor plummeted past them and crashed through the bottom of their boat. A plume of water went up, like the spume from a blowing whale.

Several of the sailors leaped for the gunwales of the sloop; Creighton and Peter quickly dispatched them with belaying pins. The rest dived into the water and swam for shore.

With every inch of sailcloth raised, they managed to come about and drift toward the mouth of the bay. Though their progress was agonizingly slow, by the time a British gunboat had hoisted its huge sails and set out after them, they were in the open ocean and heading for home.

━━━◆◆◆━━━

Chapter TWENTY-THREE

*W*hen Peter learned that the man he'd been hauling about with him wasn't Washington, he showed no surprise. "I fought alongside the general, you know. I'm not sure I could have carried him so easily; he was nearly as tall as I am."

Though he was saddened by the news that Washington had been hanged, that didn't surprise him, either. "I suspected all along that the Brits would consider him too dangerous to live."

Under the influence of the sea air, Harry Brown seemed to improve a little—at least enough to reproach Creighton for risking his own life to save him. "You promised you'd leave me behind."

Creighton shrugged. "I lied."

"You gave me your word of honor. Doesn't that mean anything to you?"

"It would have, once. But I've learned that honor is not measured by words; it's measured by deeds."

When it became light enough to see, Arnold said, "We need to dig that bullet out of your leg."

Creighton grimaced. "I know." The only surgical tool at their disposal was the dagger. While Arnold cleaned and sharpened the blade, Creighton fortified himself with several shots of rum.

Arnold offered the knife to Creighton's father. "Perhaps you'd rather do it."

"My hands are shaking too much," Harry Brown said. "You go ahead."

Peter handed Creighton a leather sailmaker's palm. "Bite down on that."

The ball was even more agonizing coming out than it had been going in. Though Creighton tried hard to bear it in silence, when the knife blade entered the wound, he let out a howl that was muffled only a little by the leather between his teeth. Thankfully, Arnold was quick about it. When the ball was out and the wound drenched with rum and bound with cloth, Creighton slumped back on the deck, sweating and gasping.

Arnold put the ball into his hand. "A souvenir. It wasn't in deep; you'll be dancing jigs inside a week. You're fortunate that it was a pistol and not a musket."

"When you hear old soldiers talk about the glory of battle," Creighton said weakly, "you never hear them mention how much it hurts."

Arnold gave a sharp laugh. "Of course not. If they did, we'd have a devil of a time finding new recruits."

Harry Brown's remission was short-lived. By afternoon he was quaking with chills again. "He needs a dose of Peruvian bark," Arnold said. "We'll put in at Pensacola."

"Are you sure that's safe? You're a wanted man there, remember."

"I don't plan to pay a visit to the governor's mansion."

Once again they waited until nightfall to enter the harbor. Arnold set off in the dinghy alone. When he returned an hour later, he handed a small packet to Creighton, without leaving the boat. "Give him a pinch of that each day. You'll want to mix it up in a glass of rum; it's bitter as gall."

"Aren't you coming aboard?" Peter asked.

"No. Our ships will be here in two days. I'm going to gather the Patriot sympathizers together and see how much mischief we can do in advance."

Creighton stared at the general. "You mean to go ahead with the attack?"

"Of course. Why wouldn't we?"

"Have the British sent any of their troops to Mobile, as you planned?"

"No."

"Then their garrison will be at full strength."

"It can't be helped. Our fleet is already on the way."

"Perhaps we could intercept them."

Arnold made a scoffing sound. "It's been difficult enough to get the Patriots and the Spanish to agree on a course of action. Now that they have, I have no intention of trying to talk them out of it. Peter, I think it's best if you stay with the sloop and help get her back to New Orleans. I doubt that Creighton can manage her single-handed—or single-legged, for that matter."

It was too dark to see the expression on Peter's face, but the disappointment in his voice was obvious. "Oh. I was hoping that—"

"Those are your orders, Corporal."

"Yes, sir." Peter reached over the rail and held out a hand to the general. "Good luck to you."

Arnold didn't respond. He stood a moment, looking up at them. Then abruptly he took up the oars and rowed off into the darkness.

"Was he angry with you?" Creighton asked.

"No," Peter said. "With himself, more likely."

"With himself? Why?"

"I don't know, exactly. Maybe because he an't able to say what's in his heart."

They sat listening to the plash of oars until it faded. Then Creighton said, "We'd better sail out of here, before we find ourselves in the middle of a battle."

The quinine powder helped Harry Brown's condition a good deal. He was still weak, but the fevers and chills no longer racked his body. By evening he was strong enough to take a short turn at the tiller.

When Peter went forward to stow the anchor rope, Harry Brown said quietly, "He seems disappointed to be missing out on the fighting."

"I know," Creighton said. "It's curious; he's such a good-natured sort, you'd think he'd find it painful, having to kill another person."

"Soldiers quickly learn not to regard their adversaries as people; they're just the Enemy."

"Then why . . ." Creighton hesitated.

"What?"

"Why did you carry a warning to the Americans? Why didn't you just let them be slaughtered?"

"You think I was wrong to?"

"No," Creighton said. "I only wondered."

Harry Brown took a long time in answering. It wasn't as if he was uncertain what to say, but as if he was deciding how best to say it. "We're all accustomed—not just soldiers, but all of us—to thinking that there are two sides to every conflict: our side and the other side. By definition our side is right and theirs is wrong. But after a few months in the army, you discover the truth of the matter: The sides keep changing. One year the Spanish—or the French, or the Americans—are on our side, the next they are our enemies. And if there's no real distinction between our side and theirs, then it becomes impossible to separate right from wrong, winner from loser. In a war there is only one line that can be drawn with any certainty: the one between the living and the dead." He sighed wearily and handed the tiller over to Creighton. "So you see, when I warned those settlers in Carolina, I wasn't choosing the American side over the British. I was choosing life over death."

It took them three days to reach New Orleans. Creighton saw no sign of the American and Spanish fleet along the way. When they anchored the sloop in Lake Pontchartrain, they hailed a small boat whose owner took them up the bayou. Harry Brown was still too weak to walk on his own;

Creighton and Peter fashioned a stretcher out of spars and sailcloth and carried him on to the city.

Rather than take his father to the military hospital, Creighton preferred to tend him personally, with Sophie's help—assuming that Sophie was still speaking to him. They found her in the printing shop, which had risen miraculously from the ashes. She was sitting at a newly constructed table, placing squares of type into the composing stick.

When they entered, she glanced up and nearly dropped the stick. "Peter! Creighton!" She sprang to her feet and ran half a dozen steps toward them before remembering her rules of behavior. She halted and performed a curtsy. "I am pleased to see you both in good health." Then her downcast eyes took in the bandage around Creighton's calf and grew wide. "*Bonté!* You are wounded!"

"It's nothing much," Creighton said, embarrassed. "My father's far worse off than I."

"Your father? *Mais*—I thought he was—"

"He's alive, but very ill. I was hoping you could spare a room for him."

"Of course! Where is he?"

"I took the liberty of putting him in my old room."

"*Non, non.* Put him in Dr. Franklin's chambers. He'll be more comfortable. Besides, you will need your old room for yourself."

"Oh? I didn't know—I wasn't sure whether you'd . . . whether I was . . ."

Sophie seemed amused at his obvious discomfiture. "Do not worry. This week I am practicing *le pardon* . . . forgiveness." She spun about suddenly, waving a hand at the restored shop. "How do you like it? *Les Patriotes* came to my aid, and in only three days it was all *comme nouveau* . . . like new." She sniffed distastefully. "Except for the smell of smoke."

Peter examined the printing press. "This actually survived in working order?"

"*Oui.* They had only to replace the *poutre* . . . the beam on the top, and the handle."

"What about the types?"

"Some of them melted, I am afraid. But we can still print the newspaper, if we are careful to avoid words with *F*s and *G*s in them."

"*We?*" Creighton said.

"*Oui,*" replied Sophie.

Creighton laughed. "No, no, I mean *we* as in *us.*"

She gave him a hurt look. "Did you not mean it when you said you would help me?"

"Of course I meant it." A few months before, he would have been horrified at the prospect of working as a printer. But since then his ideas, both about work and about the nature of a gentleman, had changed considerably. "Do you really suppose we can manage it, without Dr. Franklin to guide us?"

"I am certain of it," she said firmly. Then she added a bit sheepishly, "My virtue for last week was resolution."

"How many more weeks," Peter asked, "before you've gone through all the virtues?"

"*Eh bien,*" Sophie said, frowning thoughtfully. "That depends."

"On what?"

She smiled slyly. "On how long it takes me to master *humilité.*"

Creighton learned that the fleet had departed for Pensacola only two days before. The big vessels must have sailed farther out to sea than the sloop had—probably to reduce their chances of encountering any British ships. A week went by, then two, and still there was no word from the fleet, no indication of whether the attack had succeeded or failed.

At last a Spanish merchant vessel arrived from Havana, with the news that the Spanish and American forces had been routed. Half their ships had been destroyed; the other half had fled south to the Spanish-held island of Cuba, where they were repairing their vessels, tending to their wounded, and burying the few bodies that hadn't already gone to a watery grave in Pensacola Harbor.

In an alehouse, Creighton located two English-speaking sailors from the merchant vessel. He bought them drinks and interviewed them at length, hoping to learn enough about the battle and its aftermath to write a report for the newspaper. One of them, an American, had talked with a fellow Yankey who lost an eye in the fighting.

"According to this fellow," the sailor said, "they never had a chance. The British eighteen-pounders blew them to pieces."

Creighton's head had begun to throb again. Closing his eyes, he pressed his fingertips against them and waited for the pain to pass. On the screen of his closed eyelids, all the scenes of violence he had witnessed these past weeks seemed to unfold again, like some macabre shadow play. Beneath the pounding of his own pulse in his ears, he seemed to hear the cannonballs ripping through the rigging of the *Amity*, the agonized cries of the wounded, the rasping voice of his dying uncle, the mosquitolike whine of musket balls.

"Are you all right, mate?" the sailor asked.

Creighton opened his eyes and took a deep draught of ale. "Yes. Tell me, did you happen to hear anything about the fate of Arnold, the American general?"

"Aye, I did. This fellow I spoke to said that the general got out alive, but that one of his legs was shattered by grapeshot, and had to be cut off."

Creighton sat up long after dark that evening, attempting to write a coherent account of what he had learned, but the right words seemed to elude him. The few sentences he managed to put down on paper were as inscrutable as a passage written in code. He couldn't seem to make sense of it all. Dozens of men had died, dozens more were gravely wounded, ships on both sides had been sent to the bottom or blown apart—and for what?

Even if the Spanish and Americans had won the battle, what would have been accomplished? It would only have led to more fighting, and more lives lost. What was it Dr. Franklin had written, in those pages from his memoirs? *There never was a good war or a bad peace.*

Creighton set his paper and pen aside and, taking up his candle, crossed the foyer to Franklin's old chambers, which now were occupied by his father. Daily doses of Peruvian bark had improved Harry Brown's health considerably, but he still fell prey to occasional attacks of fever or chills. Though he helped in the printing shop when he could, and seemed to enjoy it, he spent much of his time abed.

Creighton quietly opened the door and moved over to Franklin's desk. The pages the old man had shown him lay on the desktop, anchored in place by the model of the steam engine. He sat himself and the candle down and drew the pile of papers to him. The page he had read from before still lay on top. He tilted it to catch the candlelight.

Having lived through two wars and studied the histories of countless others [it read], *I have concluded that there never was a good war, or a bad peace. It seems to me that wars are nearly always waged not for the sake of some ideal but for the sake of gain.*

Ministers and leaders of nations are, for the most part, motivated less by their concern for the good of the country, than by their own avarice and ambition. They desire more territory or fewer taxes, liberty of

*commerce or free passage upon some waterway, and
can think of no other way to obtain them than by
force.*

*These observations, I regret to say, apply even to
the late rebellion. Most of our quarrels with Britain
were not over moral considerations, but economic
ones. Like all conflicts, it was not a crusade so much
as an enterprise.*

*If wars are indeed commercial enterprises, why do
we not conduct them as such? Why do we not put
businessmen, rather than statesmen, in charge of
our diplomacy? Rather than fighting to obtain what
we desire, why do we not bargain for it? With the
millions of dollars spent on raising and equipping
and feeding and paying an army, we could have
bought our freedom from England, as a slave or an
indentured servant does, and spared our country
untold misery.*

*Instead of resolving conflicts in the reasonable
fashion of businessmen, however, our leaders prefer
to cast themselves in the role of gambler. They play at
war as though it were a great game, and risk their
money and their lives, and the lives of their people,
on a roll of Fortune's dice.*

Why, Creighton wondered, were they wasting their time
printing in the newspaper accounts of battles, petty proc-
lamations from the government, and announcements of
theatrical performances, when there were words and senti-

ments like these lying about unread? This, not the so-called news, was what they should be reproducing for people to read, not just in New Orleans, but all over the Colonies and the western territories. Tomorrow he would speak to Sophie about it.

Creighton placed the paper carefully on the desk, as though it were a freshly printed page of type. As he did so, his hand brushed against a deck of cards, the one Dr. Franklin had used to gull Creighton into working for him.

He picked up the deck and, without thinking, laid out two rows of cards, six to a row. He sat gazing at them a moment, wondering why he had done this. Then he remembered. When he was much younger, before he had become so enamored of the game of Hangman, he and his classmates had been inordinately fond of a simpleminded game called War. The two players each formed a rank of six cards—the line of battle. Only the knave, king, queen, and ace were armed. After one player's royal cards had fired a volley, his opponent removed the dead soldiers—the cards that lay in the line of fire. Then he replaced them with new ones and fired a volley of his own, and so on, until one side had lost all his cards.

It seemed a harmless enough game, on the face of it. The disturbing thing was that it reflected the way he and his fellows felt about actual warfare. Just as they considered hanging a form of amusement, they considered war a sort of great game, as Franklin put it, rather like an enormous duel, governed by a set of rules that ensured that everyone played fairly and honorably.

But Creighton had lately come to see duels and battles in a different light. They were not something to be played at; they were deadly earnest. And they were not subject to rules or codes of honor; combatants did whatever must be done in order to prevail.

Creighton picked up one of the knaves and studied it. Perhaps it was only a trick of the light, but the expression on the knave's face seemed somehow insolent, devil-may-care. It put him in mind of his drinking companions back in Bristol. They had treated all of life as though it were merely an extension of the card games in which they endlessly engaged. Once, Creighton had wanted nothing more than to be dealt in, to be an accepted, accomplished player of the game, a gentleman who squandered his money and his days and, at the end, had nothing to show for it, or less than nothing.

Creighton heard his father stirring, and he cupped one hand around the candle flame, hoping to keep the light from waking him. But Harry Brown sat up and said groggily, "Creighton?"

"Yes, Father."

"What are you doing?" He leaned forward and peered at the cards spread out on the desk. "Playing a game?"

"No, sir," Creighton said, and began gathering up the cards. "Not any longer."

Author's NOTE

ny reader who has studied much American history will have a fairly good sense of what parts of this book are based on reality. For example, most of you will—I hope—know that the British did not, in fact, win the war. But when it comes to the finer points of the story, you may be unsure just how much is true and how much is my own invention.

Creighton is entirely fictional, of course. So are Colonel Gower, Harry Brown, Lieutenant Hale, Captain Pierce, and Sophie. The character of Peter is modeled after a real-life person—Peter Francisco, a Continental soldier who, in 1776, was fifteen years old and six and a half feet tall. Legend has it that he once lifted and carried around a 1,000-pound cannon.

As you're probably aware, all the other Patriots mentioned in the book really existed. Benedict Arnold and

Benjamin Franklin were, in real life, pretty much the way I've presented them. Neither ever lived in New Orleans, so of course Franklin never published a newspaper there. Nor did he print a subversive paper called *The Liberty Tree*. But he was a successful printer in Philadelphia, publisher of the *Pennsylvania Gazette* and the famous *Poor Richard's Almanac*.

Most of the sayings I've attributed to Franklin were his actual words. Though he truly did write an autobiography—and it's well worth reading—it doesn't include the passage that appears near the end of this book. That was assembled from bits and pieces of Franklin's other writings and reworded to make it read more smoothly and logically. As for whether or not Franklin invented window screens and the evaporative cooler—well, all I can say is, if he'd lived in New Orleans in the summer, he surely would have invented them.

Though most of the events in the book are fictional, a number of them are variations of real events. Dr. Franklin's account of Washington's capture by the British is completely accurate—except that the general was rescued by his men at the last moment.

Aaron Burr actually did propose that the western territories secede and form a separate nation; in fact, he was put on trial for treason as a result, but not until 1807. Spanish forces really did invade British territory, two years later than it happens in the book. But far from being defeated, the Spanish captured all the British forts in Florida, including the one at Pensacola.

Is it fair to take such liberties with the facts? Perhaps not in a straight historical novel. But *The Year of the Hangman* falls into the category of *alternate history,* also known as *uchronia.* The whole point of an alternate history novel is to play with the facts a bit, to explore what might have happened if certain events in history had turned out differently. If you'd like to learn more about alternate history, or want to read other novels in the genre, there's a Web site devoted to it at www.uchronia.net.